Star Mage Exile

Star Mage Saga Prequel

J.J. GREEN

ISBN: 978-1-913476-06-9

ALSO BY J.J. GREEN

SHADOWS OF THE VOID SERIES

SPACE COLONY ONE SERIES

*CARRIE HATCHETT, SPACE
ADVENTURER SERIES*

LOST TO TOMORROW

THERE COMES A TIME
A SCIENCE FICTION
COLLECTION

DAWN FALCON
A FANTASY COLLECTION

CONTENTS

Sign up to my reader group for free books, discounts on new releases, review crew invitations and other interesting stuff:

https://jjgreenauthor.com/

CHAPTER ONE

Carina slung her Jensen 31 across her back and crawled beneath the remains of a desk. She had to bend low to avoid snagging the weapon on broken wood. The door to the room was slightly ajar, and from outside came the whispers and hisses of pulse slugs and the stamp of running, booted feet.

She hated hiding in the middle of a firefight but if she didn't do something soon, it would be all over for her and her merc band, the Black Dogs.

Easing into a spot where she was hidden from view, she bit on the fingers of her silicon mesh glove, pulling it off. She dropped the glove and worked on the other until both her hands were free. Removing her protective gear was reckless, but she needed bare fingers to tell if the wood splinters from the desk were real. If they weren't, the Cast would not work.

Of course, casting brought its own risks. She faced slavery and torture if anyone found out what she was about to do. Not for the first time, she wondered whether being a mage was more of a curse than a blessing. On the other hand, saving her and her merc buddies' lives would be a definite benefit.

The door banged against the wall as it flew open and someone burst in. A pulse fizzed and a body hit the floor. She peeked from underneath the desk. A fellow merc was lying flat on his stomach and facing away from her, a smoking hole at the weak point where his helmet connected to his body armor. The man trembled once then was still.

Though she couldn't see his face, she recognized the dead man. It was the latest recruit, his new career cut short by the suicide mission they'd been sent on.

Another figure ran in. Carina saw the calves and boots of one of the attackers. She shrank backward and lifted her Jensen, resting her finger on the trigger. If the soldier looked under the desk, he would receive a pulse round in his face. But the legs turned and left, and she heard footsteps running up the stairs to the next level. It was a lucky escape, but her luck wouldn't last much longer.

She picked up a splinter of wood from the desk and rubbed it between her fingertips. After peering closely at the fibrous strands, she closed her eyes to concentrate on their texture. The wood fibers were fine but not fine enough, and they were too smooth. The wood was fake. She threw down the splinter in disgust.

Her canister of base elixir was missing only one essential element: wood. The real stuff had proven hard to find on this desert planet. Of course, even if she found some natural wood to add to the elixir, it was no guarantee she would be successful. There had to be fifty or more enemy soldiers in the embassy. She'd never cast at so many, but she had to try.

Crawling out from under the desk, Carina scanned the room. Before it had been blown apart, the place had been luxurious. Some kind of animal skin buffed to a fine sheen had covered the walls, though now it hung in tatters. A delicate translucent mineral, intricately carved, had supplied the window lattices. Broken pieces of it were sprayed over the floor.

The room must have belonged to a high-up embassy official, maybe even the Matahman ambassador—the kind of official to own real wood artifacts.

The sounds of the struggle for possession of the embassy were growing louder. Fighting was going on in the stories above and below. Skirting the body of the fallen recruit, Carina closed the door and went over to a cabinet. The door was secured, but a single pulse from her Jensen melted the lock. She levered the door open with the muzzle.

Reaching inside, she riffled through bottles of the local liquor, beakers, hard copies of documents, expensive-looking jars of some kind of local food or ointment, and boxes of different sizes. Carina pulled out the boxes and tried to open them, but they were fastened shut in a way she couldn't figure out—possibly DNA or electronic locks.

She had no time for cracking fancy locks, neither through ingenuity nor casting. After a brief glance at the door, she stood and brought the butt of her Jensen down hard on one of the more fragile-looking cases, smashing it apart.

Her luck seemed to be holding. Inside the case was an oblong object. From the complex design carved at one end, she guessed it was some kind of seal or stamp. More importantly, the artifact displayed the finely grained effect of wood. Carina drove down the butt of her Jensen again, the blow jarring her arms.

She'd split the seal at one end. Squatting, she dug her fingers into the split and ripped the object apart. She extracted a thin splinter and rubbed it into fine strands.

From outside came the sound of footsteps running downstairs. No time remained to figure out if the seal was natural wood and not another clever synthetic. Carina took out her canister of elixir, unscrewed it and dropped in the strands. She swirled the mixture once, brought it to her lips and swallowed a mouthful.

The elixir was foul-tasting, as usual, but Carina barely registered the taste anymore. Her eyes were closed and she was already writing the ideogram in her mind, willing herself to ignore the steps that were drawing closer.

Creating the character required the utmost concentration. The Cast was useless unless the strokes were completed perfectly and in the correct order. One after another they appeared in her mind's eye.

Just as she drew the final stroke, someone ran in. Carina's eyes flew open and grabbed for her weapon, which was slung over her shoulder, but the newcomer was merc officer Lieutenant Torres.

"Come with me, Lin," the lieutenant said. "Up to the—"

Torres fell forward, the back of her

helmet a ruined, burning mess. She squirmed at Carina's feet. Behind her, framed by the door, was the enemy soldier who had shot the lieutenant at point blank range. His weapon was now aimed directly at Carina. She didn't stand a chance. The soldier grinned.

Then the Cast began to work.

As always, the effect wasn't immediate. If the soldier had ignored it and fired, Carina would have been dead, but he was distracted by its sensation. The man hesitated, his weapon still pointing at her, and looked down at his arms in disbelief as they began to disappear.

He lifted his head to meet Carina's gaze, his grin quickly giving way to a look of panic. The next moment, he was gone.

And so were most of the rest of the enemy in the embassy, Carina hoped. She estimated the Cast's radius to be around forty meters, which had to encompass most of the enemy within the building.

She dropped to her knees at Torres' side. The woman was no longer moving, and Carina's stomach turned at the sight of gray matter oozing from the split in her helmet. Gently, she turned the lieutenant over. Her eyes were fixed and still.

Mourning the lieutenant, the new recruit, and whoever else had died on the hopeless assignment would have to wait until later. It was time for the Black Dogs to retreat before enemy reinforcements arrived.

Carina listened hard for sounds of fighting, but the embassy was quiet. Her Cast had given the mercs a little breathing space. She went to find the rest of her platoon. Speeding downstairs, she leapt over the corpse of a fallen attacker and empty steps before running into the embassy lobby. She skidded to a halt. Three Jensens were aimed at her.

"What the hell do you think you're doing, Lin?" barked Captain Speidel, lowering his rifle, "I nearly shot you."

His rebuke stung, though Carina knew in his eyes she deserved it. She had a lot of respect for the captain and hated being the object of his disapproval.

"*Are* we under attack, sir?" asked Staff Sergeant Brown. "The ones who had me and Halliday pinned down vanished. And I don't hear any fighting. Did you see what happened to the enemy?"

"I'm not sure what I saw," Speidel replied.

"Sir, Lieutenant Torres bought it," Carina said. "And the new guy too."

"Shit." Speidel turned away to speak into his helmet mic. As she listened in to his conversation with the mercs on the upper stories, Carina heard their confusion about the sudden disappearance of the attackers. The mercs on the roof reported more enemy forces approaching from every side.

It didn't need to be said. If they didn't get out of there soon, they were screwed.

CHAPTER TWO

The soldiers crammed into the shuttle that would take them back to their starship, *Duchess*. They laid the bodies of the fallen in sections under the floor. *Sleeping in the locker,* it was called.

No one said a thing while the shuttle lifted into the air and away from the embassy, which was now ripe for the taking. The atmosphere was tense as the mercs waited for ground-to-air fire while they made their escape, but nothing came. The enemy seemed to have lost interest now that they'd retreated. Carina guessed it would be some time before the reinforcements realized that their associates had disappeared. It would be still longer until the soldiers she'd transported returned from the spot where she'd sent them.

She was mind-weary after such a large Cast. She was also worried about the questions that would inevitably be asked about the unusual events of the firefight. In the two years since she'd joined the Black Dogs, she'd kept her Casts small, personal, and easily concealed. It had been the first time she'd risked doing something so noticeable.

After the shuttle left the danger zone, there was none of the banter and jibes that usually went on among the mercs at the end of an mission; none of the black humor they employed to deal with the loss of friends and even enemies within their band. They'd failed. They'd retreated, and ingrained into the men and women, who were mostly ex-military, was the shame that came along with that.

The mysterious disappearance of their attackers hadn't yet been mentioned, as if no one wanted to risk being thought mad or stupid. Carina was certainly not going to be first to bring it up.

The merc sitting next to her, Smitz, reached into a pocket and pulled out a wad of the foul herb he was addicted to. He bit off a few centimeters of the brown substance and pushed it into his cheek with his tongue before beginning to chew. Carina immediately regretted her choice of seat.

She shifted her boots sideways in case he targeted his spit near her feet.

"Bastard lied to us," Smitz finally said, breaking the silence.

The Black Dogs' assignment had been to act as back up for the government force that was supposed to be defending the embassy, only the government troops hadn't shown.

His comment was met with mutterings and grumbles. Captain Speidel, who was sitting next to the exit and gazing out of a small porthole, didn't seem to have heard Smitz's words.

"Can't fight a company with a platoon," Smitz continued, drawing further murmured agreement.

"Quieten down, soldier," Speidel said, finally noticing the man's complaints. The murmurs ceased, and the captain returned to his morose contemplation of the view.

Carina felt for Speidel. He would be the one to take the blame if the top brass decided after debriefing that he'd made the wrong call, despite the hopeless situation they'd found themselves in.

He was a good man who didn't deserve the shit thrown at him as the meat in the sandwich between Tarsalan, the company's owner along with commanding officer Cadwallader, and grunts like Smitz. Carina was, and always would be, grateful to

Speidel for saving her from persecution and squalor in the slums of a nowhere planet. Though she rarely admitted it to herself, the older man was the closest thing to a father she had. She hoped he wouldn't suffer Tarsalan's ire, though it was unlikely he would be so fortunate. The woman was notorious for her fixation on profits and disregard for the lives that were lost to achieve them.

Still no one was mentioning what was on everyone's mind—that all the attackers within the embassy building and compound had suddenly, inexplicably, vanished.

In the end, it was Halliday who spoke. "Hey, did...er...did anyone see anything weird happen down there?"

The uneasy shifting of bodies was the soldiers' only reply. Even Smitz, who was never slow to tell everyone and anyone exactly what he thought, was silent on the issue. From the corner of her eye, Carina could see Speidel shaking his head, no doubt wondering how he was going to explain to his superiors that the only reason most of them had gotten out alive was due to an impossible event.

The micro-gravity of low orbit was taking hold, and Carina lifted from her seat and bobbed against the straps of her harness. They were nearly back at *Duchess.* Soon, she would be able to return to her cabin and safely stash her canister of elixir away from prying eyes.

"Hey, Lin," said Smitz. "You got any water? I'm all out."

Thinking that if he didn't chew his disgusting herb he wouldn't be so thirsty, Carina shook her head.

"Come on, Lin. Don't hold out on me. We're nearly back at the ship."

"Then you can wait," Carina replied.

"Come on, give me some. I know you always bring extra. I can see your bottle sticking out like a third tit." Smitz made a grab for the pouch that held the elixir canister. Carina deflected his arm with her elbow, following through and driving it into his gut. The blow had no effect other than pushing him away a little, due to the man's armor. Smitz reached out with his other hand and Carina knocked that away too. She shoved him into the bulkhead for good measure.

"Smitz. Lin," barked Brown. "Cut it out, or you're both on report."

Smitz relented. Carina's racing heart slowed, and she was glad that her face was hidden behind her tinted visor. Her skin was hot and moist with sweat.

It was with relief that she felt the shudder that rippled through the shuttle as it engaged with *Duchess'* access hatch. After another few moments she was pulling herself through the short tunnel that led to the ship. As she went along, *Duchess'* AG field took hold and Carina's feet drifted to the floor. She let go of the bars she'd been grasping and walked.

Now that they were back at their ship, the chances of reprisals for the mission went down. *Duchess* didn't live up to her name in terms of classy looks, being rather dumpy and squat, but she more than made up for the deficit with armaments. State-of-the-art pulse cannons fore and aft and fusion-rocket long-range missiles were supplemented by turret-mounted rail guns. As well as deterring space pirates with cocky ideas, *Duchess'* artillery meant that retaliation from the opposing side after a mission was rare. When it came to Tarsalan's own safety, she didn't skimp.

The same could not be said for the mercs. Carina and the others removed their armor and hung it up in the armory. The protection was flexible, light and tough, but it was showing signs of wear. At the embassy, their attacker's weapons had been able to penetrate it at close range. One of the problems of working as a merc was that levels of technological advancement varied widely between worlds. New weapons were constantly being developed, and they were never quite sure what they would be up against next.

Carina transferred her canister from its pouch into her shirt and went straight to the cabin she shared with three other mercs. It was empty. She slid the canister into the hole she'd dug in her mattress. Then, finally relaxing for the first time since she'd cast, she lay down on her bunk and put her hands behind her head. After around half an hour a comm woke her.

"Corporal Lin," came the message. "Report for debriefing immediately."

Her earlier tension returned. Why did they want to talk to her? Had someone seen what she'd done? Carina wondered how that might be possible, and her stomach dropped as she remembered that Lieutenant Torres had been wearing a body cam like they all did. What if it had recorded her casting?

She swung down from her bunk, wracking her brain for an explanation as to why she would have taken a drink and then stood still with her eyes closed in great concentration, just before a horde of enemy soldiers disappeared.

By the time she reached the debriefing room, she hadn't thought of a logical explanation for her behavior.

CHAPTER THREE

"We don't need to know everything," said Lieutenant Colonel Cadwallader. "Only describe exactly what you saw toward the end of the engagement, Corporal. Don't leave anything out."

Standing to attention in the mission room, Carina's gaze flicked to Captain Speidel, who sat on one side, stroking his stubble and watching. Cadwallader and Tarsalan sat behind a desk.

Cadwallader's pale blue eyes seemed intent on piercing right through her, and Tarsalan's full lips, coated in a purple sheen, were set in a line. Neither gave a hint of what they were expecting her to say. Carina didn't know if she had to explain herself regarding Torres' body cam footage or only report on the disappearance of the enemy.

She hesitated.

"We don't have all day, Lin," Tarsalan said, her heavy-lidded eyes drooping lower. The woman drummed fingers bearing thick, bejeweled rings on the desktop.

"Around ten minutes before Captain Speidel gave the order to withdraw," said Carina, "I was alone in a room. I think it might have been the ambassador's office."

"What were you doing there?" Cadwallader asked.

"Checking for insurgents, sir."

"Go on," said Cadwallader.

Carina explained how Lieutenant Torres died. "After the lieutenant fell, the enemy turned his weapon on me," she went on. "He would have shot me too, except..."

Her mouth was suddenly very dry. She swallowed.

"Spit it out, Lin," said Cadwallader, frowning.

"Whatever you saw, or thought you saw," said Speidel, "all you have to do is tell the truth."

Carina focused on the captain. "The soldier disappeared, sir. Right in front of me. One minute he was there and the next he was gone."

Tarsalan gave a huff of bitter frustration. "Just like the others. This is ridiculous."

"We have the body cam vids," said

Cadwallader. "They don't lie."

"It was an optical illusion," said Tarsalan.

"All fourteen of them?" Cadwallader asked.

"It makes no sense otherwise," Tarsalan countered. "If someone's invented cloaking technology for individuals, why didn't they use it when they attacked? Why use it in order to retreat, especially when by all accounts they had the upper hand?"

"I don't think it was cloaking technology," said Cadwallader. "I think it was something else."

"Like what?"

The lieutenant colonel was about to reply but he noticed that Carina was there, still standing to attention.

"You're dismissed, Corporal," he said.

Carina saluted and left. She guessed her story backed up the testimony given at earlier debriefings. She hadn't been singled out for scrutiny, but Cadwallader's comment that the soldiers' disappearance had been *something else* had her stomach in knots again.

The sound of fast-moving footsteps from behind made her stop and turn. It was Captain Speidel, striding quickly to catch up to her.

"We're going in the same direction," he said. "Let's walk together."

As a subordinate, Carina's compliance was a given. The two continued on their way.

"How are things going for you?" Speidel asked.

"Pretty good, sir."

"You can drop the *sir* for the moment, Carina."

"Okay." Speidel had talked with her in this friendly way fairly regularly since recruiting her to the merc company, and she enjoyed their amiable conversations.

"I wanted to give you a heads up," Speidel went on. He put a hand on her shoulder. "Stop a moment."

Carina turned to him.

The man's expression was serious and pained. "You can't tell anyone else what I'm about to say to you. I can trust you, right?"

She nodded.

"Why am I even asking?" Speidel smiled. "You're tighter than a drum." He checked up and down the empty corridor. "I wanted to let you know, things might be over soon for the Black Dogs. We might be disbanding. So if you come across an opportunity to do something else, you should probably take it."

"Disbanding, s...?" She stopped herself just in time. "Why?"

"Tarsalan's been complaining for a while

now that she's pouring creds into the company and making no profit. This last job we just did might be the final straw. The client's refusing to pay the balance of the fee because the embassy was taken."

"But they lied," Carina exclaimed. "We were on our own and totally outnumbered. We could never have defended the place. If we hadn't withdrawn, we would have been slaughtered."

"That's not what they're saying at their end. But it doesn't matter what they say. If they won't pay, they won't pay."

"Maybe Tarsalan should send us on a mission to persuade them," Carina said bitterly. Working with the Black Dogs was her life. She didn't know what else she could do. She was damned if she would join the military and get paid a pittance.

Speidel gave a wry smile. "That might be effective one time, but as soon as word got out we'd never work again. It isn't like merc bands are difficult to find these days."

"So you're saying I should sign up with another company?"

"I don't know. Soldiering's a tough life. Maybe you should try something different while you're still young and it isn't burned into your bones. The galaxy's a big place. There has to be some way for a young woman to make a living that doesn't put her life on the line. You aren't dyed-in-the-wool military like most of the rest of us."

Carina shook her head. "Fighting's all I know."

Speidel sighed and resumed walking. Carina went along with him.

"I sometimes wonder if I did the right thing," Speidel said, "breaking up that fight you were in and signing you up as a merc. You might have ended up doing something less dangerous and more worthwhile."

"No. I wasn't gonna win that fight. I took two of them out, but I was five minutes from being beaten to a pulp. If you hadn't stepped in..." Carina's memory of the event was vivid. Though she'd learned her fighting skills the hard way over the previous six years since Nai Nai died, even she was no match for the five boys who had set upon her. Their motive was only to have some fun, it seemed, as she had nothing to give them. It was a heavily bruised, bleeding Carina that Captain Speidel had brought back to *Duchess* and patched up. "Well, I wouldn't be here now, that's for sure.

"If you take my advice," Speidel said, "you won't be here for much longer." The captain's comm button chirped. He checked the message. "Looks like my dinner will have to wait. Think over what I said, Carina. It might be time for a change."

As the captain turned to go back the way he'd come, Carina thought she saw a look in his eye that indicated he knew more than he was saying. She felt sick. Had the captain's friendly advice been a cover for a deeper warning? Had he guessed her secret, and did he think that others were also drawing closer to the truth about what had really happened in the embassy fight?

Perhaps it was indeed time for her to move on.

CHAPTER FOUR

None of Carina's bunk mates had returned to the shared cabin, so she took advantage of the rare moment of solitude to meditate. Nai Nai had taught her the habit, telling her that it preserved and strengthened one's powers.

The old woman had said that though mage abilities were genetically inherited, it wasn't a fixed thing like hair or eye color. Casting was also a skill that had to be learned, refined, and maintained, and she'd explained that if Carina didn't regularly perform mental exercises, her ability would lessen and perhaps fail. What was more, if she did lose her ability, there was no guarantee that it would ever return once she was an adult, no matter how hard she worked.

Sitting in her top bunk, Carina crossed her legs and faced the wall. The steps to achieve a trance state were always the same. She mentally recited and embraced the concepts of the five Elements: wood, fire, earth, metal, water. Following the Elements were the Seasons: spring, early summer, late summer, autumn, winter. This second part of the pre-trance task was not so familiar to Carina. Though she'd visited many worlds while working with the merc band, she'd never encountered a place where the climate followed the pattern laid out by Nai Nai with its types of weather, variations in temperature, and fluctuation of daylight hours.

Next, she mentally wrote the Strokes. Each line had to be written perfectly, each taper and flourish correct. She wrote them separately and then together in the character that meant *forever*. Finally, she conjured up the Map in her mind. Nai Nai had made her draw the 3D image over and over again on her holoscribe while she was growing up. There were more than a hundred stars, and her grandmother would measure the angle and distance between each star carefully when she finished. If anything was incorrect, she had to draw it again.

The Map showed the birthplace of their clan, Nai Nai had said. At the center of the Map was the star system that their ancestors had been driven from, so long ago that no one knew when.

Carina had once asked her grandmother why they didn't try to return to their original home.

"No one knows where to go anymore, Mei Mei. No one remembers where we came from."

"But we have the Map," Carina had persisted. "Why can't we find it using that?"

Nai Nai had laughed and dipped her hand into a jar of sand she used for polishing the beautiful stones she sold for a living. She scattered the sand across the floor where Carina sat.

"Tell me, Mei Mei, how many grains do you see?"

Carina frowned. Was it a test? "Ten thousand? No. Fifty thousand."

"Probably about five thousand. Look closely, child, and imagine these are stars. In our section of the galaxy alone there are ten times as many stars as there are grains of sand lying here. It would take several lifetimes to visit each and check if the surrounding pattern of stars matched the Map. One would need to look at the groupings from many orientations. And our galactic sector is only one of thousands."

The young Carina eyed her holoscribe drawing, which had taken her over two hours to create. "Then why bother remembering it at all? Why not give up on ever returning home?"

"That is something every mage must answer for herself. But let me ask *you*, little one, do you feel as though this place where we live now is your home?"

Carina considered their two-roomed house, which in truth was little more than a shack. She considered the dirty street outside with its open gutter that kept the local rats well fed. She considered how different she felt from the other children, who didn't know the Elements or the Seasons or the Strokes or the Map, and who could not cast. She shook her head. "I don't, Nai Nai."

The old woman sighed. "My great-grandparents told me once they'd heard it said that our birthplace was the origin of humanity itself—the world where humans first evolved, invented space travel, and journeyed out to colonize new planets. If we could find that place again, it would truly be something very special.

"But more important even than that, the Map gives us hope," her grandmother continued. "we are exiles and our clan has been scattered to the stars. Nowhere are we accepted for being who we are. We live in secrecy, always. The Map holds the promise that one day we may live openly and together again in our homeland. Holding onto that possibility helps us to go on."

Remembering Nai Nai's words calmed Carina's anxiety a little, and she slipped into a deep meditative state.

Some time later, the sound of the cabin door opening entered the edge of her consciousness. She brought herself out of her trance and turned to see Thyrna Atoi, her bunk mate, bend down to sit on the lower bunk. She began to take off her boots.

"You missed dinner," said Atoi. "Not that you missed much. Chef's on a marine plant kick. Yeuuuch! *It's high in nutrients and protein*, he said whenever anyone complained."

"I wasn't that hungry anyway," Carina said.

Atoi threw a boot at the corner of the room. "Got it!"

"What was it?" Carina asked. "A roach?"

"Yep," said Atoi as she went across the room to retrieve her boot. She picked up the squashed insect by a leg and carried it to the garbage disposal chute.

"That's not a roach," Carina said. "That's a scalobite."

"What difference does it make?"

"Scalobites are good. They eat roaches."

"Whatever. Now it's a dead scalobite."

Carina sighed and lay on her back. The bunk shuddered as Atoi shifted her position. She was a large, heavily muscled woman.

"You missed the announcement too," she said. "Got another mission. Hykara sector."

"Where's that?"

"Don't know. A long way from here. We're fast-burning through the quiet shift."

As Atoi mentioned the fast burn, Carina began to feel the vibration of *Duchess'* engines powering up. She lay down and fastened the safety webbing over her bunk. Soon, the ship would lurch as they switched to FTL drive.

"What's the mission?" Carina asked, studying the rust patch in the corner of the ceiling above her bunk.

"Search and rescue. Kidnap victim."

"Huh? Isn't that one for a planetside control force?"

"You'd think, wouldn't you?" Atoi replied. "Word is, no one local will touch it. *Other mercs* won't touch it. We're only doing it because it's that or disband. Tarsalan says she'll pull the plug otherwise."

Unfastening her webbing temporarily, Carina leaned over the edge of her bunk to look at Atoi. The woman had the satisfied expression of someone spinning out a juicy piece of gossip.

"What else does the word say?" Carina asked.

Atoi smirked. "The boy who was kidnapped is a Sherrerr, and the kidnappers are—"

"Dirksens," Carina finished for her. She threw herself onto her back. "We've bought it."

"Yeah. Everyone's trying to bail but Tarsalan won't let them. Says they have to work out their contracts. No negotiation. After the last mission, people were already pissed. Some chairs got thrown, tables broken. Tarsalan exited at the first sign of trouble and left Cadwallader and Speidel to calm things down."

Carina could imagine the scene. She was glad she'd skipped dinner. Merc bands were mostly made up of men and women who had left—or been discharged from—the military because they were unstable or lacked the discipline necessary for service in the forces. They could be aggressive, anti-social, impulsive, and belligerent.

Her soldier buddies' personality quirks had never bothered Carina much. Surviving alone on the streets from a young age had brought her into contact with many unsavory types. In fact, the mercs' unpleasant characteristics made things easier for her. Superficial friendships and casual hookups were all she could risk in terms of relationships. In her time with the Black Dogs, she'd only ever contemplated something more with one man: Stevenson, the shuttle pilot, who was relatively sane. She'd avoided him ever since coming to the realization.

No, mercs were not to be messed with, and Tarsalan, in her usual nonchalant, disinterested manner, had just told a room of them that their next mission was to be even more suicidal than their last.

CHAPTER FIVE

As Carina went to the armory to suit up before leaving on the mission to rescue the little Sherrerr boy, she was reconsidering her decision to go along. Speidel had advised her to move on from the merc band, and she had recently come dangerously close to revealing her ability. What was more, the assignment was highly risky. Even if they succeeded—which wasn't likely—the chances were that the Dirksens wouldn't rest until it found and punished the people responsible for thwarting their plan. And in the list of possible punishments the Dirksens meted out, the best and rarest option was a quick death.

Despite Tarsalan's threats, there wasn't much the company owner could do to the mercs who refused to take part in the assignment other than fire them. Being let go was a problem that paled in comparison to the potential consequences of defying the Dirksens.

The Sherrerr/Dirksen feud was notorious. It had gone on for so long, the inciting event was lost in time, but the reason for their mutual hatred and constant clashes didn't matter. The Sherrerrs and Dirksens were equally wealthy, powerful, and corrupt, which meant that their rivalry to be the ruling clan in that sector of the galaxy was inevitable.

Anyone with any sense had nothing to do with either family if they could help it. It was true that when you were on the inside, you had access to all the luxury and privilege the connection provided, but there was a large drawback: you could never leave. Once you were in, you were in for life and that was that. If you left, you were an unacceptable liability, and you would spend the rest of your prematurely shortened life looking over your shoulder, wondering where and when the blow would fall.

Carina guessed that the Sherrerrs had promised Tarsalan rich rewards and lifelong protection for her and her loved ones to persuade her to take the deal. The same recompense and safeguarding wouldn't apply to the grunts who did the actual work.

The mercs who had refused the job were dumped on a remote planet, unpaid. The rumor was that Speidel had threatened to resign, though for some reason he was now coming along. Perhaps his motivation was similar to Carina's. She certainly had no interest in the clan feud or in incurring the vengeful spite of the Dirksens, but she had thought more than once about the little boy they had taken.

According to the information the Sherrerrs had given, he was only six. Carina had been but four years older when she had also found herself alone with no one to protect her, and she hated to think how the ruthless Dirksens might treat a Sherrerr they had in their clutches. No ransom note had been issued, and no other explanation had been given for the kidnapping, so what they were planning to do was unclear.

Someone had to get the boy out. Carina had done some morally questionable things during her time as a merc. If rescuing an innocent child was to be her last mission, it would be a fitting finale to her career.

The armory was already busy with the rest of the mission squad. She took down the legs of her armor and stepped into them, tightening the fit before slotting the torso into place and sealing it. The arms came next. She slipped the canister of elixir into its pouch and adjusted its position so that it wasn't in the way. From the edge of her vision she noticed Smitz watching. She gave him the stink eye and bent down to pick up her helmet.

"Hey, what are you doing, you bunch of useless grunts?" asked Captain Speidel as he appeared at the door. "Didn't you hear the directive? If we go in there dressed like soldiers, we'll be blown to bits before we get within five klicks of the target. You're in civvies for this. And no guns. We don't want to draw any attention when we disembark. We'll buy weapons planetside. Get changed and get to the shuttle. We're leaving at eleven hundred and fifteen."

Half an hour later, Speidel gave them a final briefing as they descended to the planet.

"Listen up," he said to the eight mercs seated on each side of the shuttle, looking uncomfortable in normal clothes. "Orrana's a young world, geologically speaking. Too young to be settled, in my opinion. It's highly volcanic, and while that makes for lucrative mining operations, the effects are pretty much what you would expect on a relatively new planet: regular eruptions, earthquakes, tsunamis, geysers, boiling volcanic springs, and so on.

"The biggest settlement is on one of the

most stable landmasses, and it's a pretty lawless place from what I can gather, which suits our purposes perfectly. That sword cuts both ways, however. If anyone gets into trouble, they only have themselves or us to rely on to get them out of it. There is a local civil control force but it's probably either ineffective or crooked. It's unlikely to interfere in any fights and we might find ourselves on the wrong side of it if it becomes known why we're there. If they don't already know what the Dirksens are doing, they probably aren't going to do anything if they find out.

"You're likely wondering how we know where the Dirksens are holding the victim. The simple answer is the boy's been fitted with a transmitter. It's embedded in him, so we have his exact coordinates. We only have to break or sneak through the Dirksens' guard, rescue the lad, and escape with him. *Duchess* will be ready to run the moment we have him aboard."

Smitz said, "You left something out, Captain."

"What's that, Private?"

"What's our cut and when do we get it?"

"What?"

"The Sherrers must be paying a fortune to rescue their kid. What I want to know is, how much of that cred are we seeing?

What's our bonus?"

"No one's mentioned a bonus, Smitz."

"We're taking all this risk so Tarsalan can buy another pretty ring?"

"You'll get what you're paid," said Speidel. "Now be quiet."

"Right," Smitz said. "I'll remember that when the Dirksens have me cornered in a dark alley. I'll be sure to give them her home address." He spat into the gully that ran down the center of the small ship.

Speidel grimaced in disgust. "What the hell are you chewing, man? Hand it over."

His face set in anger, Smitz pulled out his packet of herb and gave it to Speidel, who put it in his pocket.

"Take these," Speidel said, handing out breathing masks. "Wear them at all times and never breathe the local air. The atmosphere has enough oxygen, but the CO_2 level will kill you. I'm hoping we won't have to stay the night there, but if we do, change the filter every day. Everyone take one of these too." He opened a drawstring bag containing small electronic devices. "They're comms with high level encryption, as you won't be wearing your helmets."

Carina took one of the small gadgets and pushed it into her right ear. She pulled her hair forward to cover it. When Speidel spoke again, she heard his voice loud and clear.

"Now I know we don't do much plain clothes work," the captain continued, "so some of you might not feel comfortable with it. What you have to try to remember is that, until we're inside the place where they're keeping the kid, you're to try to forget that you're soldiers. Whoever's guarding the child will be on the lookout for anyone who seems like they could be ex-military."

Pondering the captain's words, Carina's gaze roved over her fellow operatives. Smitz was the largest of the bunch. He was built like a heavyweight fistfighter and wore a permanent scowl. Brown was as tall as Smitz but more supple and lithe. He moved like a predator. Next to Brown was Atoi, who loved to work on her upper body strength. Her bull neck and biceps were stretching the material of her shirt.

On Carina's left sat Carver. She had a scar that ran diagonally across her cheek and under her nose, permanently lifting her top lip. It wouldn't have been expensive to get the scar fixed, but Carver seemed to like the look. Halliday sat on Carina's right. He had the gaze of someone who had seen enough horror for several lifetimes. Further on from Halliday were Jackson with his prosthetic arm and Lee, who had a nervous tic that made him blink excessively.

They were gonna buy it for sure.

CHAPTER SIX

They set up at a hostel for transient workers while Captain Speidel went out to procure some weapons. Firearms of any kind were prohibited on the planet according to the signs at the arrivals section of the spaceport, but it seemed as though no one paid much attention to the rule. Carina had seen guns and rifles carried openly as they rode the transport to the hostel.

Orrana was a dark place in climate and mood. Thick haze generated by frequent volcanic eruptions blocked much of the sunlight. As a result, vegetation was minimal. Deep gray-green, straggly stems covered the black soil to the horizon. Speidel had told them that animal life was at the microorganism stage, so they had nothing to fear from the indigenous species.

Carina doubted the same could be said for the Dirksens or their employees.

The locals that she'd seen at the spaceport wore sour or suspicious or desperate looks, judging by what she could see of their faces. Their breathing masks covered the nose and mouth and were fastened by a strap on each side of the face and one over the top of the head. The clothes the locals wore were basic and utilitarian and their hair was plainly cut. Fashion was not of any importance on Orrana. Survival was.

The mercs' story was that they were a team of smelting workers. It was a subterfuge intended to account for their rough, burly appearance. If asked, they were to say that they were looking for work and were not interested in setting up their own operation. Conflicts over land, mining rights, and raw materials were rife, and the mercs were to expect scrutiny in that regard.

As she stood in the shared hostel room and pulled tight the wide belt she wore, she hoped that no one would ask her any awkward questions. She didn't have a clue about smelting.

Atoi stepped into the room. "Come downstairs," she said. Her voice was muffled by her mask, but the comm Carina was wearing conveyed the woman's words.

"Speidel's back. We're leaving soon."

Carina caught her reflection in a mirror as she left. She so rarely looked at herself in a mirror, let alone saw herself in civvies, that she paused a moment to take in the sight. She was wearing narrow pants that went down to her calves, boots that fastened with interlacing straps and a plain, open-necked hemp blouse. Speidel had told them to stick to dark colors.

Her figure was athletic but not bulky, and she didn't—yet—have that hard, intense expression that a life of killing had given so many of the others. Of all the squad members on the mission she thought she looked the least like a soldier. Perhaps she could find another way in life after rescuing the little boy.

Did she look anything like a smelting worker? She didn't think so, but her outfit would have to do.

She followed Atoi downstairs to the hostel bar, where the others were hanging out. Speidel wasn't there, and they were drinking the local brew. When Carina sat down at the table, someone pushed a beaker of frothy liquid in front of her. The smell of it told her the drink was some kind of alcohol. When she hesitated to try it, Jackson leaned over and said, "Speidel said it's okay. Just one drink."

For the benefit of eavesdroppers, they weren't to use the word 'captain' in public, nor any other terms that might identify them.

Carina sipped the deep green liquid. It tasted like someone had fermented the local vegetation, which was probably the case. "I think I'll pass," she said, pushing the beaker away.

Smitz laughed. He grabbed her cup and drained it.

Speidel came into the bar carrying a bulging bag. He set it down on the table and handed out weapons. Though the bar was full of the hostel's patrons, no one took any notice. It was as though on Orrana *not* carrying a weapon would be strange behavior.

Jackson held up his gun to examine it. "Where are these from? The last century?"

Smitz snickered and poured himself another drink from the pitcher.

"That's what's available at short notice on the street." Speidel held out his hand to take the gun back. "Unless you'd rather go without?"

"No, no. Not complaining," Jackson replied, pushing the weapon into the back of his pants under his shirt. "No way. Just asking."

After quickly checking it over, Carina

tucked hers into her belt.

Speidel said quietly, "I picked up some explosives too. C8 with delay fuses. They weren't difficult to find and they'll probably prove useful. They have thirty-second and two-minute delays. Okay, let's pay a visit to a smelting plant. I've hired one of the local transports. We'll talk more about the job on the way."

He clearly didn't want to risk their conversation being overheard at the bar. The eight mercs rose and left with the captain, making their way outside. As they went to where the transport was parked, Carina got her first close-up look at the settlement. She wasn't impressed. The place reminded her of where she'd grown up.

Like Carina's birth planet, Orrana was far from the center of the action and way off trade routes, and it showed. No one was planning to settle there, so no one had made any effort to create a proper infrastructure, like good roads or basic public services. From the flimsy pre-fabricated buildings to the dim street lights hung on makeshift poles, everything was temporary.

She pondered the advisability of building a smelting plant on a planet that was prone to earthquakes, but the financial savings of refining the ore planetside probably offset the costs of rebuilding after a shock. The risk to the workers was undoubtedly low on the list of priorities, as it always was in ass-end-of-the-galaxy places.

Carina climbed aboard the multi-person transport Speidel had rented. The heavy vibration when he started it up signaled that the vehicle ran on some kind of organic fuel. Orrana really was about the most backward place she'd ever been. She slid into a window seat and rubbed a clear patch in the grimy window with the edge of her sleeve. Speidel input the destination and the transport pulled into the road.

"The smelting plant where the Dirksens are holding the kid is at the edge of town," Speidel said once they were on their way down the potholed street. "We're going to pretend we're looking for work. Gangs of transients looking for labor are common. The guards shouldn't be too suspicious at first. Don't forget that you're supposed to be contract laborers. Low-skilled, boneheaded grunts."

"Sounds about right," Carver said, her scarred top lip rising in a gruesome grin.

"That way, no one's going to expect us to answer any difficult questions," Speidel continued. "All we need is enough of a cover story to get inside the plant. Here are the plans."

He handed out thin, transparent sheets.

"The red dot is the kid."

Carina studied the blueprint of the plant. It felt weird to not see the image on a visor overlay and not to be able to interact with it. The smelting plant was large and complex, and the Dirksens had secreted the boy on a basement level at its heart. As she saw the scale of the complex, the desperate nature of their attempt began to hit home.

The Dirksens had chosen the place to hold their hostage well. Not only was the boy in the least accessible part of the complex, the place was full of people working for Dirksens: tough men and women who had led hard lives. They wouldn't be averse to using their fists or whatever weapon came to hand to do their boss' bidding, and there had to be hundreds of them.

"You've gotta be joking, sir," said Lee, staring at the blueprint. His nervous tic had started up. Normally quiet, the man's outburst signaled the dismay the rest of the troop was no doubt also feeling.

"Lee's right," said Smitz. "They aren't gonna let a bunch of strangers in even if they believe our story, and if we try to fight our way in, we're dead. With our regular armor and weapons, we might stand a chance, but with these antiques, we'll never make it. Stop the transport and let me out. I'm going back to the ship."

"You'll stay right where you are, soldier," Speidel said.

Smitz spat a brown, greasy ball of spittle at Speidel's feet and got up to leave. The captain rose and roughly pushed the man back down into his seat. The soldier scowled and was about to stand again when Carina said, "Wait. What if we try something different?"

Smitz hesitated then buckled under the captain's glare.

"Like what, Corporal?" Speidel asked.

Carina outlined her plan. It would spread the mercs thin, and they would have to sacrifice force of arms to diversionary tactics and speed, but she couldn't see how they could retrieve the boy otherwise.

Speidel listened, his face betraying neither approbation nor disapproval.

"I'll go in to do the rescue," Carina added. "The kid's only six, and I think I'm the least scary of all of us. We don't want to frighten him into trying to get away. I'll need just one other person to come with me."

Atoi said, "I'll do it."

"Okay," said Speidel after a moment's pause, "we'll do it your way, Lin. It sounds like it might work."

CHAPTER SEVEN

Speidel stopped the transport two klicks from their destination and spent some time studying the smelting plant from afar. One of his eyes was an implant that had around ten times the capabilities of its biological equivalent.

While the captain was studying the processes of the plant and the movements of its workers, Carina checked her weapon over again. It was fully powered, but that was about all it had going for it. Jackson's earlier estimation that their guns were from the previous century seemed optimistic.

Her firearm was single pulse only, and the gauge on its side indicated that it had to build power between each discharge. Great. She hoped it didn't take long. What wouldn't she give for her trusty Jensen 31. Consulting with Atoi, she was relieved to find that the woman had received a better model. Hers didn't require time to recharge unless after rapid fire.

"Okay." Speidel turned around in his seat to face them. "The heap of ore on the right side is fed by a conveyor belt into a press to crush the rocks. Another belt takes the crushed rock inside—I'm guessing to furnaces to smelt it. We need to get some explosives onto the belt that enters the plant. That should mess the place up pretty good. Our second target is a pile of smoking waste on the far side of the complex. Nothing like falling red-hot ashes to rain on someone's parade.

"Another possible target is one of the chimneys. They're wide and they aren't that tall. Seems like concern for the environment is a concept that hasn't arrived on Orrana just yet. Someone with a good aim might get lucky. Anyone want to try?"

"I'll do it, sir," said Jackson. Lee and Halliday slapped the man on the back. With his prosthetic arm, Jackson was the obvious candidate.

"Good," Speidel said. "They've just turned on the lights, but their coverage isn't good. Should be plenty of shadows for cover. Brown and Carver, you're on target one. Halliday and Lee, you're on target two.

Smitz, you're with us."

Smitz gave Speidel a surly glance but said nothing.

It was nearing twilight as the transport drew close to the plant. The emissions of its chimneys were dark gray against the deepening sky, leading from a dim glow at their bases. The mercs were well beyond the edge of town, driving down an empty road.

At a dip where the transport was briefly out of sight of the complex, Speidel stopped the vehicle again, and the five mercs who were to provide the diversions got out. They immediately stooped to grab handfuls of dirt. After mixing the dirt with a little water from their canteens, they would rub the resulting mud on their faces and exposed skin, helping them to melt into the encroaching darkness.

Speidel held out his weapon to Carina. "Take this and give me yours."

Carina pulled her pulse gun from her belt. "Why, sir?"

"Never mind why, Corporal, just do as you're ordered."

She took the captain's gun and briefly studied it before slipping it into her belt. His weapon was a better model than hers. He was swapping with her relic so that she could protect herself better.

A few moments later, the transport was

on its way again, leaving the five disembarked mercs behind and slowly heading toward the light that glared from the guards' office at the main gate.

The figure of a tall woman could be seen sitting at a desk behind translucent, scratched plexiglas as they drew up. Carina glanced at the gates to the facility, which were large, heavy, and well-secured. There was no way they would be getting through them. Their only way inside was via the guards' office. She could see a shadowy exit at the back, blurred by the degraded glass of the window.

The guard was alone in the small room, her head turned toward a bank of roving holos that showed the activity inside the plant. She looked over as Speidel leaned out and spoke into the intercom. "We're here to see the manager about some jobs."

The woman's brow furrowed. "What's your name? I don't have any record of an appointment."

"You wouldn't," Speidel said. "We're only here to ask."

"The manager's busy," the woman said. "Check the job updates in the town news or make an appointment." She returned her attention to the holos.

"It would only take a minute to comm, ma'am," said Speidel. "We've got plenty of experience between us. Been working—"

"Get out of here," exclaimed the woman.

While Speidel dragged out the conversation with the guard, Atoi, Carina, and Smitz slowly opened the door on the side of the transport facing away from the guards' office and slipped out. Bent low, they crept around the vehicle and took up positions on either side of the window, just below its sill. All three had their gazes fixed on Speidel, waiting for his signal.

The captain raised his pulse gun, and they stood as one and fired at the plexiglas, cracking and melting the panes. Smitz drove his booted foot through the remains of the window on his side and Atoi elbowed out the rest. Carina followed them as they leapt into the room. The tall woman backed into a corner, her face pasty. The weapon she held was shaking. Clearly, she was just an ordinary guard and not one of the Dirksens' hired goons.

Speidel had also jumped inside. He took pity on her and fired a stunning shot. The guard slid to the floor as more appeared through the doorway at the back of the room. These men and women were professionals. They came out firing aggressively, but they weren't suited up. Carina, Smitz and Atoi picked them off with accuracy, showing none of Speidel's mercy.

The mercs' position was dangerous. They had to avoid being pinned down in the outer office, trading shots with the Dirksen thugs while the local security force made its way over. They had to force their way inside, but stepping through the door wearing no armor would be suicide.

Still, they probably only had to wait a few more moments...

A boom split the air and the floor shook. Klaxons sounded. Someone had succeeded in placing a diversionary explosive.

Smitz and Atoi ran into the rear room, spraying pulses as they went. Carina and Speidel were hard on their heels. Two Dirksen hands were on their backs in the further office, their chests smoking. Speidel hit the arm of another who reached out from behind a cabinet to take a shot and Smitz finished her off. A fourth ran down the corridor leading from the room. Atoi shot him in the back.

They sped out and into the interior of the complex. The klaxons were still blaring, the sound penetrating Carina's skull. Another boom shook the plant. The general employees would be well-occupied at least.

Speidel took the lead as they ran deeper into the building. They fired at anyone who approached. Most of them ran away. The mission seemed to be progressing well, but

Carina began to feel a nagging doubt about what was happening.

The captain took them down a set of stairs, along a corridor, and then downstairs once more. The sound of the klaxons grew quieter as they moved away from the busier sections of the complex.

"Okay," said Speidel, drawing to a stop at the top of a third set of stairs and panting. "We're here. Lin, Atoi, don't take too long. We can't hold off a sustained attack."

Carina and Atoi were to retrieve the Sherrerr child while Speidel and Smitz protected their rear. The two women ran quietly down the stairs. Though the klaxons were fainter there, Carina guessed the noise was sufficient to cover the sound of their footsteps. They were heading for a small room—not much bigger than a closet—in the corner of a large basement at the bottom of the stairs.

What they might expect to find, she didn't know. She hoped that the child didn't have a large, round-the-clock guard, but it seemed unlikely that the Dirksens would station lots of thugs right outside the kid's door.

At the top of the final flight of stairs, Carina and Atoi stopped. They checked their weapons, looked each other in the eye, nodded once, and bounded down the final steps, firing into the basement as they went.

The wide, low room was full of old, dusty, broken bits and pieces of equipment, lit up by the pulse flashes from the women's weapons. Carina couldn't detect any returning fire. The two split up and ran for cover behind separate hulking pieces of machinery.

Carina sat with her back to a machine and waited, listening. The room was dark, but she could see Atoi's position from the glowing dial of her pulse gun. The faint light shining from the stairs to the next level was the only other source of illumination.

No movement nor sound of any guards could be heard. Carina reached out and took a wild shot. No response.

"Atoi," she whispered into her comm. "I think the place may be empty."

"I was thinking that too," came the woman's response.

"Let's head round to the room where they have the kid," Carina said.

"You got it."

Carina crawled cautiously around the edge of the dark room, making her way to the door in the corner. Atoi approached it from the other direction. Carina arrived first. She reached upward, feeling for the door handle. She found it and pulled it down.

The door was unlocked. It swung open

easily. Something was very, very wrong.

The smaller room was also dark. Carina stood and brushed the wall next to the door until she found the light switch. As it activated, Atoi arrived.

"What the hell?" the woman said as she saw the room. Aside from a few pieces of furniture, it was empty.

"What is it?" Speidel said over her comm. "Report, Lin."

"The kid isn't here, sir," Carina replied. "I think we're in the wrong room."

"If you're in the small room off the basement," said Speidel, "that's definitely where the child should be. I'm receiving the signal from the transmitter. Are you sure you're in the right place?"

"Yes, sir," Carina said. "But the whole basement is empty. Not even any guards."

Atoi had moved into the room. A couple of overturned chairs and a small, low table were its only furnishings. "I guess it's possible the kid was here but they moved him when we burst into the plant."

"The captain's receiving the signal from here," said Carina. "The kid has to be around somewhere. But where?"

Atoi was crouching down, looking at something she'd spotted on a stained part of the floor. "Aw, fuck." She stood and backed away, the color draining from her face.

"What?" Carina asked.

Atoi raised a hand to her eyes and shook her head. She didn't answer.

Carina went over to see for herself. She picked up the object for a closer look. Her stomach lurched and her legs turned weak.

It was a tiny chip, around the size of a baby's fingernail. Like the floor where it was lying, the chip was stained brown. The stains were dried blood, and the chip was the Sherrerr child's transmitter.

CHAPTER EIGHT

Carina forced down the bile that was rising in her throat. She'd seen plenty of blood and death in her time, but she couldn't imagine how anyone could harm a small, innocent boy.

As she gazed at the tiny chip in her hand, other things started to add up until finally it all made sense. The whole mission has been too easy. They should never have made it that far with their shitty weapons and no armor. "Sir, we found the boy's transmitter. I think it was put here to lure us in. It's a trap. The Dirksens want to capture us."

She waited for Speidel's reply, but none came. Perhaps he was distracted.

"Captain?" Nothing. "Sir?"

A loud *crunch*.

Carina turned to Atoi, her eyes wide. "We have to get back to them."

They flew out of the room and across the large basement, steering around the shadowy shapes of discarded machinery in the dim light from the doorway. Atoi gave a cry as she ran into a piece of equipment low down on the floor. She tumbled over it and landed on her face. Carina ran back and helped the woman to her feet. Blood was flowing from her nose and dripping off her upper lip, dark in the dim room.

She drew her sleeve across her face and spat. "I'm okay."

They climbed the stairs together, slowly. Carina hadn't heard a sound from the captain since his most recent words to her, and there had been no sounds of fighting from the next level. But then, pulse fire wasn't noisy and she wouldn't have expected to hear it above the continuing noise of the emergency klaxons.

They crept around a corner in the stairwell and found themselves staring down the muzzles of guns.

The two guards who were waiting for them were kitted out more like Carina would have expected from employees of the Dirksens. They were dressed in full armor and bearing gleaming new weapons of a kind she'd never seen before.

Their order didn't need to be verbalized. Both Carina and Atoi put down their guns in one slow, measured movement. One guard led the way while the other went around behind them. The group climbed the stairs to the corridor, where Carina was relieved to see that Speidel was still alive. She even felt a mild satisfaction that Smitz also wasn't dead.

He was facing the wall next to the captain. Two of the Dirksens' thugs were holding weapons to their heads. Carina and Atoi were pushed against the wall next to them.

"Which one of you was it?" Atoi asked between her teeth.

"Shut up," said a guard.

"Which one of you held the kid down?"

Speidel looked from Atoi to Carina, a curious expression on his face.

The guard raised his voice. "I said, shut up."

"Who was it that dug it out of him?" Atoi yelled.

The guard fired, and Atoi screamed as a thread of light shot from the weapon and made contact with her back. She fell to the ground, writhing and jerking in agony. The guard kept his finger on the trigger, seeming to enjoy the spectacle. When he finally stopped firing, Atoi lay motionless, barely conscious and covered in sweat. Next to her was the captain's comm, which had been ground to pieces.

"We have orders to try to deliver you all alive," the guard said to her, "but the Dirksens won't mind if we slip up once or twice along the way. I was just playing with you then. Don't make me use the lethal setting."

He nodded at another couple of guards, and they hauled Atoi to her feet and pushed her against the wall once more. She swayed and staggered as she struggled to stand upright, gripping the wall with both hands.

The Dirksen thugs seemed to be waiting for something. From the corner of her eye, Carina saw the one who had tortured Atoi murmuring into his helmet mic.

Tense seconds ticked past. Carina wondered what the new weapons were that the Dirksens had. Pulse guns fired bolts of concentrated energy that burned the target or, at a lower setting, shocked him into temporary unconsciousness. The Dirksen guns seemed to emit a continuous flow of power that kept the victim in constant pain. Perhaps the lethal setting would stop the heart. She wondered what range the weapons had.

The men and women guarding the mercs were growing agitated and throwing glances from side to side along the corridor. Something was up. One of the women jabbed Carina in the back, and she gasped as the hard metal muzzle drove into her spine, causing a sharp jab of pain.

"Move," the woman said, jerking her gun to the right.

The other mercs were being pushed in the same direction. It seemed a good time to stage an escape attempt. Once the Dirksen thugs had secured them somewhere, getting away would be a lot harder. But Carina couldn't see how any of them could make a move without being immediately shot with one of the torture weapons.

The klaxons had finally stopped, and the lower levels of the plant were quiet as they went along. Carina was at the end of the line. A muzzle was thrust into her again, hitting her kidney. She bit back a yell.

"Faster," said the guard.

Carina imagined what she would do to the woman if she got a chance.

A *whompf* of detonation came from the corridor up ahead, the explosion deafening her. Cracks appeared in the ceiling and walls. Carina swung her elbow upward into the guard's helmet, toppling the woman. She snatched her weapon from her and fired. The thread of intense light shot out, but the woman only jerked in pain. Her armor seemed to absorb some of the energy.

The guard snatched at the muzzle and

tried to stand. Carina pushed the weapon against the woman's chest and fired again. That time, the guard's body spasmed and was still.

"Fire against their armor," Carina shouted, her ears still ringing from the explosion.

An agonizing flame shot through her, but was cut off abruptly. She turned to see Smitz grinning and pulling his weapon away from the helmet of a falling Dirksen guard.

Three of the mercs who had planted the diversionary explosives came running down the corridor, shooting. Carina ran at a Dirksen thug who was about to return fire. She thrust her weapon against his back and pressed the trigger.

Speidel and Atoi were struggling with their captors. The captain screamed. His guard had shot him in the eye. He fell, clutching his face. Brown ran up and body-slammed the guard, at the same time relieving him of his firearm.

"Press it up against his chest," shouted Carina.

The third Dirksen thug died.

Carina was wondering if they should try to take the fourth alive when Atoi killed him. It was the one who had tortured her.

Brown was helping Speidel to his feet. The captain's face was a ruined, blackened mess, but he was alive. The staff sergeant pointed down the corridor, in the opposite direction to the area of the explosion, and the mercs began to run.

Carina's hearing was gradually returning.

"There's a hole in the fence north-north-west, where the chimney exploded," Brown said. "If we get split up, make for it and head back to town. We'll meet at the back of the hostel. We leave for the shuttle at 0600."

He didn't say it, but the implication was clear. Anyone who didn't make it to the rendezvous point in time would be left behind.

CHAPTER NINE

Things were turning ugly aboard *Duchess*. The five mercs who had set the explosives had encountered Dirksen guards roaming the complex, and neither Carver nor Lee had survived. Brown, Halliday, and Jackson had fared better and headed to find out what had happened to their captain after they heard the fateful *crunch* of his comm.

Setting a small explosion in one part of the corridor provided the distraction to give the mercs the edge they needed to turn the tables on the Dirksen thugs. After escaping over what remained of the fence, the surviving mercs had eventually made it to the shuttle and returned to their ship.

That was where the shitshow really started.

Carina had always known that Sasha

Tarsalan was a nasty bitch, but she'd never witnessed the level of fury the woman unleashed on the mercs who had failed their second mission in a row.

The heavily bejeweled woman ranted and raged at the six mercs, spittle flying from her mouth. Speidel was in the sick bay, where the ship's doctor was removing what remained of his ocular implant. Carina and the others stood to attention, facing the full brunt of Tarsalan's fury in silence.

'Incompetent' and 'inept' were among the nicer words she used to describe them. According to her assessment, they were also 'moronic grunts,' who were a 'waste of oxygen' and had 'brought the company to ruin with their pathetic efforts.'

After a while, as Tarsalan explained how 'real' soldiers would have behaved like professionals and done the 'simple job' they were asked to do, Carina tuned the woman out. She watched her gesticulations, red face, and bloodshot eyes but paid little attention to what she was saying. Tarsalan's hair was piled into a tower on her head, and as Carina watched, the tower began to slip and hang at an angle. She wondered if, and when, it would fall down entirely.

The patience and stoicism Nai Nai had taught her from a young age meant it wasn't difficult for her to bear Tarsalan's dishonest, unfair ferocity. The other mercs, however, were not so well-equipped. Though none moved nor spoke, their growing rage was almost palpable.

Predictably, Smitz was the first to snap. He didn't say a word, however. He strode over to the woman and stood glaring down at her, his hands in fists at his sides and his broad, heavily muscled back tense.

Tarsalan's words dried up, and she seemed to suddenly realize that she'd spent the last ten minutes insulting and berating six professional killers, and that she was alone with them. She swallowed and looked up at Smitz. Her previously puce face paled, but she said tersely, "What do you think you're—"

Perhaps if she'd apologized, Smitz might have mastered his rage. Even if she'd said nothing at all, there was a chance he would have calmed down and stopped himself from doing something stupid. Though he was undisciplined and often offensive, Smitz had spent so long skirting the line of report-worthy behavior that he knew exactly where it lay.

As it was, Tarsalan's continued arrogant attitude made the man snap. He grabbed her throat, lifted her with one arm, and slammed her against the wall, where she hung, wriggling. The company owner's eyes protruded from their sockets and her mouth was forced open by the pressure of Smitz's hand on her neck. Her tongue waggled wildly but not a sound nor breath left her mouth.

She plucked uselessly at Smitz's fingers while her feet kicked and jerked, suspended several centimeters above the floor.

Carina and the other mercs enjoyed the spectacle for a few moments until, halfheartedly, they tried to make Smitz release his hold. Staff Sergeant Brown gave him an order to drop Tarsalan immediately, and the others tried to open his fingers and pull him away from her.

With apparently great reluctance, Brown finally fired at Smitz and stunned him. As he collapsed, Tarsalan fell to the floor too. She was unconscious but still alive. The marks of Smitz's fingers on her neck were already showing.

"Good one, Smitz," spat Halliday. "Now we're out of a job for sure."

"We were out of a job anyway," said Atoi. "If he hadn't done it, I would have soon enough. He only did what we all wanted to do."

Jackson agreed. "I would've punched her, though. Probably more than once."

"Quit it," said Brown. "Lin, help me get her to sick bay. This son-of-a-bitch goes to the brig. You understand, Atoi? Halliday? Jackson?"

The three nodded glumly. Transporting Smitz to the brig would be no mean feat, whether he was unconscious or awake.

After notifying the doctor they were on their way, Brown and Carina managed to carry Tarsalan to the sick bay between them. She had begun to regain consciousness by the time they arrived. The two of them lifted her by her shoulders and legs and put her on a bed.

Brown quickly left. He might have been avoiding Tarsalan's fury, redoubled after Smitz's attack, but the man's hand had damaged her neck to the extent that she could barely croak. The doctor told her to be quiet while he examined her and motioned Carina away. She had hung around in case the doctor wanted to know what had happened, but the evidence apparently said everything.

Carina had passed a curtained bed on her way into the sick bay. She guessed the occupant had to be Speidel. She peeked in. The captain was awake and reading an interface with his remaining eye. A patch covered the place where the other had been.

She opened the curtain wider. "Hi, sir." She spoke quietly so that the doctor wouldn't hear and maybe make her leave.

Speidel's smile when he saw her eased her concern for the older man somewhat. He put down the screen. "Come in, Carina. It's good of you to come and see me."

She stepped close to the bed and drew the curtains closed.

"Did doc get all your implant out?" she asked.

"All that was left of it," Speidel replied, pulling himself into a higher position before relaxing on his pillows. "Several thousand creds gone in a single shot. But I was lucky, really. If the beam had hit my real eye, it would probably have fried my brain. Better one-eyed than dead, huh?"

"I'd say so. Are you going to get another implant or a new bio eye?"

"I'm not sure. I guess it depends on whether I continue soldering or take the hint and retire. Have you heard what's happening with the company yet? Cadwallader isn't answering my comm and the doctor won't tell me anything, except to rest up and not worry myself for a while. Like it's easy not to worry when you don't know what's going on."

"Well..." Carina wasn't sure if she should tell Speidel about the incident with Tarsalan and Smitz, but she guessed that he would find out soon enough, what with being right next to the company owner.

"Holy shit," Speidel said when she reached the part where Smitz had tried to strangle Tarsalan. "What an imbecile. If it wasn't over for the Black Dogs before, it certainly is now. Tarsalan's definitely going to cut her losses and split after this."

"No doubt about it. Which kinda makes your advice to me earlier moot, doesn't it?"

"Yeah. But it was good advice, Carina. Brown, Atoi, and the rest will find another merc band to join. Even Smitz might find someone who's on the lookout for an insubordinate, aggressive bastard. But...listen to me, okay? I've gotten to know you over the years, and you aren't like them. I didn't realize it when I dragged you out of that fight. I never told you, but I watched it going on for a while before I stepped in. I watched you defend yourself against those older, bigger street rats, and I saw your skill and strength. But that was all I saw.

"I thought that providing you with a safe place to live and a regular paycheck was fair exchange for what you could bring to the band. And you stepped up and did the job, after a little training. It wasn't until later that I saw a different side to you. You can fight and kill if you need to, but you don't like it. You aren't immune to it like half of the others, and you don't relish it like the other half."

Speidel half shut his remaining eye, scrutinizing her. Carina began to feel uncomfortable.

"There's something else about you too. Something more than disliking the fight."

Carina felt that familiar wrenching she had whenever she was worried someone might discover what she was. Time to change the subject. She had another topic on her mind anyway.

"What's going to happen now, sir?" she asked. "About the Sherrerr kid, I mean."

Speidel sighed. "Who knows? Now that he no longer has his transmitter, it's going to be a lot harder to find him. Whatever happens, we're out of that game."

"Are we? It doesn't seem right to abandon him like that. He's just a little kid."

"He's just a little *Sherrerr* kid. If anyone has the money and influence to track him down, it's them."

"That's something I don't get," said Carina. "They're so rich and powerful, why did the Sherrerrs hire us to do their dirty work? Why not send in their own goons?"

"I never got that either," Speidel replied, "and, for what it's worth, I feel the same as you. I'm not happy about leaving the search to someone else, assuming someone else *is* searching for him. But I don't know what else we can do. He could be anywhere, and the Dirksens sure as hell aren't telling."

"That's the other thing that bothers me," Carina said. "Why did they kidnap him in the first place if they don't want to ransom him? They just took him and disappeared. What's the point of that?"

"Maybe for revenge. Maybe they already murdered him. That room where you found his transmitter, was there...?"

"No," Carina replied. "There was only a small amount of blood. Not enough."

"Whatever the Dirksens did with the kid, we've reached the end of the road. Even if we wanted to continue after Tarsalan disbands the company, we have no way of finding him."

"I guess you're right," Carina said, but inside she was saying, *Yes, there is*. She had kept the child's transmitter. The trace of blood on it held his genetic code—his unique signature in the fabric of the universe—and that meant that she could find him, but she would have to cast.

CHAPTER TEN

The doctor bought the mercs some time when it came to the breaking up of the Black Dogs. He insisted that Tarsalan remain in the sick bay and leave the running of the ship to Cadwallader for at least forty-eight hours. If the company owner had had her way, Carina was sure she would have thrown them all off the ship at the earliest opportunity with no time to pack their stuff or make arrangements.

As it was, after Smitz's attack, no one was in any doubt that the band's days were over, and they acted accordingly. The soldiers began to clear out their cabins and pack the items they wanted to take with them. Cadwallader transferred the monies owed to them to their credchips, and people decided where they would go next.

Mealtimes became almost convivial as stories of old missions were recounted, then the mood would turn melancholy as the dead were remembered. Silence would eventually fall as the mercs no doubt inwardly reflected that their fate would be similar.

Captain Speidel was up and about the day following Smitz's attack, looking more than ever the old soldier with his eye patch. The skin on his face glistened with burn-healing gel and only very pink, fresh color remained of the damage the Dirksen guard's weapon had done.

Carina was happy to see him looking not too the worse for wear, and not only for his own sake. The plight of the Sherrerr boy had lain heavy on her mind and heart ever since the failure of their mission. She had made the Cast and found the child, but the knowledge was useless if she had to attempt a rescue alone. The Dirksen force was formidable, and she doubted she could defeat them even using her special abilities.

She needed help, yet how could she convince anyone she knew the boy's location unless she explained *how* she knew it? She would have to reveal that she could cast. The thought of it alone made her break out into a sweat. Nai Nai had impressed nothing else upon her more than the fact that she must never divulge her secret. Even the idea of it felt like an act of betrayal to the woman's memory, but if she didn't do something, she would be leaving a young child to suffer—perhaps even to be murdered.

Carina was glad the captain's recovery was going well because she'd decided that, of all the people she knew, he was the one she trusted the most. He'd also expressed his concern about the missing child and he might be persuaded to help her mount a rescue.

When her cabin was empty, Carina removed the canister of base elixir from its hiding place in her mattress and went to Speidel's room. She found him alone.

"Come in, Carina. I'm glad to see you. Have you come to tell me what you're going to do next?"

She stepped into the man's single cabin and waited for him to close the door before she spoke. "I have, and I need your help to do it."

Speidel sat on his bunk while Carina took the chair. The captain rested his elbows on his knees and clasped his hands. "Would you like me to write you a reference? I'm happy to, but I'm not sure how relevant it will be if you're giving up the soldiering life as I hope you are."

"I've thought about it," Carina replied,

"and maybe you're right that I'm not suited to life as a merc. Maybe I will give it up, but it isn't over for me yet. I have one last mission I have to do. I want to rescue the Sherrerr kid."

Speidel straightened up. "I understand how you feel, but as I said, we're hamstrung on that. We don't know where—"

"I *do* know where he is. He's in the smelting plant. He was probably there all along. We were just tricked into going to the wrong part of it."

Speidel's expression was a mixture of confusion and disbelief. "But surely you're speculating. You can't know for sure, and we can't return to the plant on a guess. It's far too dangerous."

"I'm not speculating. I know where he is." Carina took a deep breath, trying to quell her racing heart. "I know because I cast to find him."

"You...?"

"Sir..."

The captain was looking concerned. Carina became even more aware of her flushing face and anxiety. Was she making the worst mistake of her life? Perhaps, but she was committed. "You must swear to me that you will never tell to anyone what I'm about to tell you. If you can't make that promise, then we can't do anything about the Sherrerr boy. It's very important that what I tell you remains a secret between us. My life depends on it."

Speidel nodded. When Carina waited expectantly, he said, "I swear."

"Thank you," Carina said. "It's a little difficult to explain, sir, but I can do things that most people can't. Things that I can't rationalize and that don't make sense scientifically, as far as I understand. Yesterday, when I was with you in the sick bay, you said there was something different about me. That's because I *am* different, though I don't know how or why."

Speidel didn't speak. He was giving her the space to finish what she wanted to say.

Carina explained how her Nai Nai had brought her up after her father died and her mother disappeared, and how the old woman had taught her to harness and hone her casting power. She didn't tell him the details like the Elements, the Seasons, the Strokes, or the Map. Those weren't necessary for the captain to know. He only had to believe what she could do and that the Sherrerr boy was where she said he was.

"It isn't a simple or easy process," she went on. "The reason I was able to cast to find the child was because I had something of his. I had the transmitter that Atoi found. I can't find people randomly, or at least I never learned how. Nai Nai died when I was ten, and I was alone after that. I couldn't fit in where I was. Maybe the people in my neighborhood could sense the same thing that you can—that I wasn't like them. I used to get picked on a lot."

She stopped. She felt she had said enough for Speidel to take on board for the moment. Oddly, though all her life she'd feared someone finding out that she was a mage, she now felt relieved, as if a burden had been lifted from her. It felt good to share her secret with someone else. She realized how alone she had felt before.

Speidel rubbed his stubble. "That's quite a story, Carina." His tone was non-committal.

Carina's heart sank. He didn't believe her.

"I take it you can prove what you say," he said.

"Yes," she replied, her hope rising. "Yes, I can. I thought of a simple Cast I can do to show you, but I don't want to unsettle you."

"I've been a merc for eleven years and in the military for thirteen," Speidel said, laughing. "I don't think there's anything you can do to unsettle me."

Carina took out her canister of elixir and sipped a mouthful. She scanned the cabin for a handy object and saw the captain's uniform hat on a table. She closed her eyes and drew the ideogram in her mind. The Cast was an easy one.

She opened her eyes to see that the captain had an indulgent, disbelieving look on his face. He opened his mouth as if about to say something to mollify her, but then his hat appeared on his head. He reacted as if a poisonous spider had just fallen on him. He threw the hat to the floor and leapt up so fast that his legs hit his bunk and he overbalanced, falling comically onto it.

Carina tried to suppress her laughter but was unsuccessful. In all the years she'd known him, Speidel had been the model of self-control. She'd never seen him so surprised or amazed.

Still lying on his bunk in an awkward pose, Speidel blinked his single eye several times. He sat up. "Well, I asked you to prove it, and you did." He straightened his pants and ran a hand through his graying hair. Reaching down to the floor, he picked up his hat and turned it over in his hands. "I guess I believe you."

"You do?"

Speidel nodded. "It's a lot to take in, but to tell you the truth, it isn't the first time that I've heard about such abilities. Of course, I never believed the stories before. What else can you do?"

"Quite a lot of things, though some are

easier than others. I can move things, as you just saw, and find things that are missing if I have a part of the object—something to link to it. I can heal, though it's difficult and not fast. I can't prevent someone who's been shot from dying, for instance. I can start fires and engines at a distance, open locks, change my appearance—"

"Can you hurt people...kill them?" Speidel asked softly.

Carina looked down and slowly nodded. "But it isn't straightforward. Shooting or knifing is much easier."

There was a moment's pause as Speidel considered her response. "Oh," he suddenly blurted, his eyes wide. "It was you! At the Matahman Embassy. It was you who made the enemy soldiers disappear."

She gave another quick nod.

"Did you kill them? All of them?"

"No. Like I said, that's hard to do. I just moved them about a kilometer away."

Speidel whistled in admiration. His brow furrowed. "I saw you drink from that," he said, indicating her canister. "Is that essential to what you do?"

"Yes. I must take a sip of elixir. And...do some other things."

"So if I drank that, would I be able to do magic too?"

A shadow settled over Carina's heart. Was

this what Nai Nai had meant when she'd said that knowledge of her abilities would turn friends into enemies? A change of direction to the conversation was needed. "I don't think of it as magic. 'Magic' sounds like something out of children's stories, like three wishes and wizards disappearing in puffs of smoke. I think my ability is natural, only it's very rare and outside our current understanding of the universe."

She paused. "Even if you had the ability, you wouldn't be able to cast just by drinking the elixir. It takes training and practice and there's a lot more involved besides." She handed him the canister. "Take a sip and try if you don't believe me."

He took the offered canister and lifted it to his lips. His gaze upon her, he tipped back his head and poured a measure of elixir into his mouth. Immediately, the liquid erupted as he spat it out, splattering it across the floor. He coughed and retched for a minute or so. Wiping his eye, he said, "You didn't tell me it tastes like weeks-old piss."

The corners of Carina's mouth twitched. "You get used to it. Are you going to try some 'magic' now?"

Still wiping his eye and mouth, Speidel burst into laughter. "Okay, you got me good. If I have to drink that sewer effluent, I'd rather stay non-magical. What's in it?"

"Nothing that's important by itself. What do you say? Do you believe I'm right about the location of the Sherrerr boy? Will you help me rescue him?"

"I do believe you. How couldn't I after your little demonstration? And I will help you rescue the child. But I don't think we should try to do it alone. I'll speak to some of the others. I'll tell them I received additional intel from the Sherrerrs. Maybe we can rope in some of them to help us. But we'll have to start soon."

"Yeah. I hate to think about that kid all alone among those thugs, especially after what they already did to him."

"Not only that," Speidel said. "I plan on us going in fully armed this time, which means we need to leave before the doctor lets Tarsalan get up."

CHAPTER ELEVEN

Somehow, Smitz got wind of what they were doing, and he insisted that he wanted to come along too.

"He's just saying that so he can get out of the brig before Tarsalan recovers," Carina said to Speidel when he told her. "The minute we arrive planetside he'll be gone."

"I don't think so," the captain replied. "There's more to Smitz than meets the eye. I would have kicked him out of the Black Dogs ages ago if I didn't think so. He talks a lot, but he always follows orders in the end. And he came on the previous mission when he didn't have to. He could have bailed like most of the rest did."

"He was expecting a bonus, though."

"And when he found out he wasn't getting one, he came along anyway. I think he wants to help."

"I don't know, sir. I don't like it."

"I've been commanding mercs for a long time. They're a difficult bunch and it's easy to underestimate their better motivations. I think you should trust me on this."

Carina sighed. "Okay, if you say so."

Atoi had also quickly volunteered when approached, and Stevenson was happy to fly the shuttle.

Scans of the smelting plant showed that the explosions had put it out of operation. The damage the mercs had caused was extensive. There was little movement and the furnaces were cooling after being shut down.

According to the results of Carina's Cast, the Dirksens had the Sherrerr boy in what seemed to be a staff locker room on the first floor. The room was central, which meant another deep infiltration from the perimeter of the building. Approaching the front entrance was out of the question. They had no reason to be there as the place had closed down for repairs, and they would be recognized immediately.

Carina's idea was to approach at night from another direction and enter the site through a breach in its fence.

"They won't be expecting us," she said. "They won't think we'll return to the same place."

"They might if they find out the intel about the kid was leaked," said Atoi.

A look passed between Carina and Speidel. "I'm confident that won't happen," the captain said. "But I have another proposal," he added. "I don't doubt that the Dirksens will have alerted the planet authorities about us. If we land at the spaceport, we'll likely be arrested on a trumped up charge. Instead, we'll catch them by surprise. We tell Stevenson to fly us right onto the plant roof. We fight our way down to the room where they have the kid, grab him, and fly right out again. They don't have any spacecraft on site to pursue us. If we're fast enough, it might work."

"What about ships orbiting the planet?" Smitz asked. He was chewing his disgusting herb again.

"If the Dirksens had a starship in the vicinity that stood a chance of defeating *Duchess*," said Speidel, "we would have been under attack by now. I'm guessing they didn't want to draw the Sherrerr's attention to Orrana by stationing one of their better ships here for no obvious reason. But that isn't to say that one isn't on its way to force us out of the area after our escapade."

"Will the roof withstand a shuttle landing on it?" Carina asked.

"Enough to not collapse," Speidel replied. "And that's all that matters for our purposes. We'll be suited up, so we'll have some protection from the heat."

No more questions were forthcoming, and time was of the essence. Within quarter of an hour, they were in the shuttle and descending to Orrana's surface.

The descent was rapid. Stevenson swept them in at maximum speed. Carina and the others gripped webbing above their heads for extra stability as the ship tilted at a forty-five degree angle. The speed lifted them out of their seats, then they were thrown forward as the pilot employed reverse thrusters hard. The shuttle dropped precipitously to the smelting plant roof.

Before the shuttle had fully touched down, Stevenson opened the ramp, and the mercs ran out onto the smoking hot roof. The door to the building was locked, but in a heartbeat Smitz burst through it and led the charge down the stairs.

The mercs' attack was so fast, the first Dirksen guards they met were taken completely by surprise. Concentrated pulse fire from the mercs' Jensen rifles was sufficient to penetrate their armor, and some weren't even suited up.

By the time they reached the second floor, the news of the attack had arrived, and they met stronger resistance. Turning a corner on the stairs, Smitz ran into a shot from one of the Dirksens' advanced weapons. He was thrown back and lay unmoving on the steps.

His chest plate bore a melted patch from the glancing hit. Carina lifted his visor. Above his mask, the man's eyes were open. "M'okay," he said. "Just gimme a minute."

While Atoi sprayed pulse fire down the stairs, Speidel started the twenty second delay on an explosive. Through her comm, Carina heard him counting down. As she helped Smitz up the steps, away from the blast zone, she mentally counted with him. *Six. Five. Four.*

Speidel set the explosive rolling down the steps and sprinted up them with Atoi.

Three. Two.

The explosion roared up toward the mercs, sending a cloud of smoke and debris with it. Having no choice but to abandon Smitz for the moment, Carina, Atoi, and Speidel hurtled down the stairs and into the blast area, which was thick with a smoky haze.

Unable to see where she was going, Carina collided with a Dirksen guard and found herself sprawling on the floor. A muzzle appeared in her vision and she grabbed it, hauling the guard on top of her where the close quarters would prevent him from firing. She tried to wrestle the gun from him.

Letting go of the weapon, she jumped up and kicked it from his grasp. The gun went skittering down the stairs, and the guard tried to go after it, but Carina jumped on his back and wrenched open his visor. She ripped off the man's breathing mask and tried to throw it, but he tackled her from behind, grabbing her around the knees. Carina's helmet hit the edge of a step. The cushioning absorbed most of the blow but she remained tightly held as the guard fought to free his mask from her hands.

Carina was lying face down, head downward on the steps and her blood was rushing to her brain. She held the mask and her Jensen under her and was kicking backward to force the guard away. Suddenly, she felt the man's full weight upon her. She wriggled out from underneath him. He was dead, his face a melted mess, and Smitz was standing over him.

They continued to the bottom of the steps, where Speidel and Atoi had their backs to a corner wall. They were at the corridor that led to the locker room and the Sherrerr child.

Speidel lifted his weapon. Carina, Atoi, and Smitz nodded, then all four ran simultaneously around the corner, laying down suppressive fire as they went. Two Dirksen guards were in the corridor. The mercs' pulses focused on the first, penetrating his armor. He fell. The second guard fired at Smitz and hit him, the shot sent the man spasming to the floor. Speidel, Carina, and Atoi turned their weapons on the remaining guard and killed him.

Speidel lifted Smitz's visor. He was dead.

His voice strained, Speidel said, indicating a door, "The kid's in there."

They burst through, expecting to meet more resistance, but the room was empty save for the Sherrerr child. A sound from the corridor drew Speidel and Atoi outside again, leaving Carina alone with the boy.

CHAPTER TWELVE

The child was smaller than Carina had expected, or maybe it was only that he was hunched in the corner of the room, his head bowed and turned to the wall. He was visibly shaking, plainly terrified.

Carina realized she was still holding her weapon ready. She slung the Jensen over her shoulder and went over to the kid. He shrank against the wall and squealed at her approach.

"It's okay," she said. "I'm here to rescue you."

The boy didn't seem to hear. He pressed himself harder into the wall and moaned in terror. He was wearing a child-size CO_2 filter mask. Carina suddenly realized how scary she had to look to him, suited up in armor and with a tinted visor covering her face.

She put down her gun and unsnapped the locks on her helmet. Lifting it off, she squatted down a short distance from the boy and held out a hand. "Don't be scared. We're here to take you home."

This time her words seemed to penetrate. The boy peeked at her from underneath an arm, and for the first time Carina saw the child's large, deep brown-black eyes.

"Carina," Speidel said, bursting in again, "what are you doing?"

The captain's abrupt appearance undid all of Carina's work at calming the boy down. He flinched and turned away again, sobbing and moaning.

"Grab him," Speidel said. "We have to get out of here."

"Okay, I'm coming." Carina put on her helmet and picked up her gun. She also scooped up the child, who wriggled and fought and bit her armor. With horror, Carina saw the cause of his terror. The boy's fingernails and toenails had been ripped off. The Dirksens had been torturing him.

Holding the struggling child firmly over her shoulder, she ran down the corridor, following Speidel's echoing footsteps. In her other hand she held her Jensen, muzzle up. The hiss of pulse rounds came from up ahead. Speidel and Atoi were in a firefight.

Carina brought down the smelting plant's blueprint on her helmet overlay and searched for another escape route. She didn't want to abandon Speidel, but taking the unprotected child near weapons fire would be insane. The blueprint was complex and she had no time to figure it out. Spying what appeared to be a different route to the roof, she turned down a narrow corridor on her left. She followed the next turning too and the next, going deeper into the complex.

The boy seemed to have gotten the idea that she was trying to help him. He'd ceased struggling and hung like a limp rag over her shoulder. He was small for his age and Carina hardly felt his weight as she ran.

She turned another corner and abruptly stopped. She was at a dead end.

"What the...?" Carina checked her visor overlay. She was sure she'd seen another corridor leading from the one they were in. Her heart sank when she saw that what she'd mistaken for a corridor was an air duct. Spinning around, she saw the access point: a square wire grid in the wall, behind which a fan whirred.

The sounds of battle were drawing nearer.

"Carina," Speidel said through her helmet comm. "Where'd you go? We have to leave. Stevenson heard from *Duchess* that Dirksen ships are on their way."

"I'm making my way to the shuttle," she said. "I didn't want to take the kid within range of fire. Give me two minutes."

"You got it," Speidel said. "Don't keep us waiting."

"I won't," Carina replied, wondering desperately how she was going to make her way to the roof in time.

Her gaze returned to the wire grid. She could melt it and the fan behind it with a pulse from her Jensen, but that would leave the metal too hot to touch, and the kid had nothing to protect him.

Carina put the child down and pulled her knife from its sheath. At the sight of it, the boy took a breath as if to scream. Carina clamped her hand over his mouth. "For the last time, kid. I'm not gonna hurt you. I'm here to take you back to your family. Now can you be quiet?"

The boy swallowed and nodded. Carina removed her hand and went to the grid. She pushed the knife blade behind it and prized the cover away from the wall. The fan was only slotted in place. Carina lifted it out and peered into the dark tunnel. The boy could fit in, but it looked impossibly small for her. She had no choice. She had to try to squeeze inside.

Hastily, she began to unclip her armor.

"Get in the tunnel," she said as she worked. The boy looked from the dark opening to her. He shook his head.

"Get in," she repeated. "It's the only way. If we can make it up to the roof, we have a ship waiting for us, but they're leaving soon."

The boy still didn't move.

"Come on," she said. "Please."

He hesitated but then finally padded on his wounded feet over to the black, square hole. With a final look at her, as if checking that she wasn't tricking him, he climbed inside. Carina had nearly removed all her armor. She unclipped the legs and stepped out of them. Crouching down to enter the shaft, she rued the fact that she had no way of reattaching the wire grid once she was inside, nor of making her pile of discarded armor disappear. Where they had gone would be glaringly obvious to anyone trying to find them, but it couldn't be helped.

She picked up her helmet and put it on. The internal gel that molded around the back of her head would hold it in place, and she needed it for light in the tunnel and comm with Speidel.

The soles of the kid's bare, dirty feet were all she could see of him. He was moving fast. Was he trying to get away from her?

"Hey," she called. "Wait up."

The feet paused. Carina was relieved. The kid seemed to trust her after all. His resilience impressed her. He'd been taken from his family, kept hostage, and tortured—tortured! What kind of sick fuck would torture a six year old? And why? Did they think a little kid had secrets worth telling? Or had they done it for kicks?

She blinked the blueprint into view again, overlaid on the inside of her visor. "Helmet," she said, "shortest route to the roof." A red line threaded through the mass of green ones. An arrow pointed at the next turn. "Go left," Carina called.

A flashing clock on the helmet display made her heart sink. Estimated time to destination: 10m 23s.

"Shit," she breathed. She stopped crawling. "Hold up," she called to the kid. Going faster wasn't going to help. She needed to think.

Somehow, the boy had managed to turn around in the narrow tunnel. His dirty, tear-streaked face, topped with shaggy hair came toward her. He hadn't yet said a word to her, Carina realized. He was probably too traumatized.

Carina was on her front, facing him. She knew there was only one way out of the situation for both of them, but still she balked at it. If the kid blabbed, she would be at extreme risk. But if she didn't do what she had to, she would be captured and killed by the Dirksens, and the boy would have lost his only possible chance of escape.

She debated trying to explain away what was about to happen, but decided to just do it. Later, she would figure out how to deal with whatever interpretation the kid made of it.

Carina reached into her shirt and brought out the elixir canister, which had been painfully squeezed between her and the metal floor of the tunnel. The boy's eyes grew round.

"Just wait a minute," Carina said. "I need to take a sip of this."

She swallowed a mouthful of elixir. "Hold my hand," she said. "You're coming with me."

CHAPTER THIRTEEN

Carina appeared in a corner of the roof at just the point she'd aimed at according to the blueprint. She was relieved to find that the boy, his eyes wider than ever, was still holding her hand tightly. The shuttle was there, and Speidel was pacing impatiently in front of it.

"Quick," Carina whispered, "come on."

She ran out a little way onto the roof. "We're here, sir."

Speidel turned. "Where have you been? And where's your armor? Never mind. Get aboard the shuttle."

He cried out and collapsed to his knees before falling forward on his face. A guard had emerged from a doorway behind him as he was speaking and shot him in the back. Carina leveled her Jensen at the guard and fired off a round that hit the man's visor. The plexiglas darkened and sagged from the blast, and the guard dropped his weapon, yelling with pain.

"Go up the ramp," Carina told the boy, who was frozen, staring at the guard who was clawing at his melted visor. She gave the child a push, and his trance broke. He ran aboard the shuttle. Carina tried to haul Speidel up, but his body was heavy and entirely limp. Turning him on his back, she opened his visor. The captain's face was still and peaceful. Her heart stopped.

Sounds blurred and her vision swam. Time seemed to slow down. He couldn't be dead. Carina blinked away hot tears that were dropping onto her visor and scanned the older man's face for any sign of life, but there were none.

"Lin, get aboard." It was Stevenson, the shuttle pilot. His words pulled her out of her frozen state. In the corner of her vision, she saw movement. More Dirksen guards were arriving.

With a terrible wrench, she let go of Speidel's body and ran up the shuttle ramp. As she reached the top, agony exploded behind her knee. Her legs collapsed. She'd been shot.

The ramp closed, and pain tore through her. Without her armor's pain-suppressing injector system, she felt the full effects of her wound. She lay on her back, trying not to scream. All she could see were the ceiling lights and the concerned face of the Sherrerr boy hanging over her.

What seemed an age later, Atoi appeared, staggering in the shuttle's rocky flight. She pressed an anesthetic gun to the inside of Carina's wrist, and the cold, cool feeling of relief flooded through her. The drug made her groggy and confused too. She said to Atoi, "Where's the captain? We forgot him. We left him behind. I have to go and get him."

Atoi placed a gentle hand on her stomach. "Stay right where you are, soldier. An auto-gurney's waiting for you."

Carina's head flopped to one side. "Where's the kid?"

"He's right here," Atoi replied.

The child was sitting on his haunches against the bulkhead, watching her. He had an inscrutable look on his face. She wondered vaguely what he was thinking. What had he made of their impossible transference from the cramped tunnel to the rooftop? He was only six. Hopefully, his young mind would find a way of explaining it away.

A low hum signaled the arrival of the auto-gurney. They seemed to have made it back to *Duchess,* though to Carina only moments had passed. Atoi stepped out of the way as the device lowered to the ground and secured Carina's neck and spine before lifting her onto its base. The hum started up again as the vehicle moved away.

Carina could see only the corridor ceiling as she was carried along.

"Hey, kid," she heard Atoi call. "Come back here."

"I want to go with her," the boy protested. They were the first words Carina had heard him speak. The pain relief was clouding her senses, and she didn't hear if Atoi relented and let the Sherrerr accompany her.

The next thing she knew, she lying on a soft medroom bed surrounded by curtains.

Carina tried to sit up, but her right leg was restrained somehow. Her memory of the mission came flooding back, along with the knowledge of Speidel's death.

She lay down and wept, her tears running down the sides of her face and into her hair. After a long while, she lifted her head and looked down her body. A cylinder of transparent plastic encased the middle section of her leg. Restorative gel filled the plastic, working on the wound she'd received. Her nerves in that part of her body were numb.

On the edge of her vision, she noticed the

Sherrerr boy was sitting down nearby. He came closer when he saw her notice him, and a pair of large, brown-black eyes stared into hers. The kid had been cleaned up and his hair was a little less shaggy.

"I saw what you did," the boy said.

Carina's chest tightened. Through a gap in the curtains, she could see the doc on the other side of the room. He didn't seem to have heard the child.

She tried to signal the boy with her eyes and lifted a finger to her lips. To her great relief, he seemed to understand the need for secrecy. He nodded solemnly and moved his chair until it was right next to her bed. He watched her face.

"We should have you back with your family soon," Carina said.

The doctor heard this. "Carina, you're awake? How are you feeling?" he asked, parting the curtains. He bent over her leg to look at it closely through the transparent gel. "Should have you back to normal in ten hours or so, and no scarring. This latest gel we picked up is very good. Stimulates your own stem cells to replace the damaged tissue. Your new skin will be as soft as a baby's bottom."

"And your little friend is still here," he went on. "I thought I told you to stay in bed," he said to the boy. "Plenty of vidgames on the system to keep you occupied."

The child lifted his hand and placed it gently atop Carina's. The hand was encased in a glove of healing gel.

"I want to stay here," he said.

The doctor grimaced as Carina lifted her gaze from the kid's torture wounds toward him. He looked as though he wanted to say more but was refraining due to the child's presence.

"I don't suppose it will hurt for you to remain with your rescuer for a little while. But if you feel odd or dizzy, it's straight back to bed with you, and you must let me know. Do you understand?"

"Yes, sir."

The doctor smiled. "You can call me Harvey, son." He addressed Carina. "Keep an eye on him for me, will you? I need to report to Tarsalan on how you're all doing."

"Is she up and around now?" Carina asked. "Has she recovered?"

"She hasn't fully recovered, no, but that didn't stop her from getting up and telling the Sherrerrs of your success the moment she heard about it. We're on our way to one of the planets they control right now."

"What's happening with the Black Dogs?" Carina asked. "Did she say anything about that?"

"You've been through a lot, Lin. Just take

it easy for now, okay? I'll be back in an hour or so." He left, pulling her bed curtains closed.

"What's your name, kid?" Carina asked, realizing that he'd only ever been referred to as the victim, the target, or the Sherrerr child.

"Darius," the boy replied. He leaned forward. "I saw what you did," he repeated.

The familiar, horrible clenching in Carina's chest returned. The boy's words also reminded her of something else she needed to be concerned about. She craned her neck to scan around for her belongings. Her clothes had been folded in a pile on the shelf next to her bed, and the metal elixir canister was on the top of the pile. A little relieved, she sunk back into her pillows.

She had to divert the child's mind to another subject. "How are you feeling?" she asked.

"I'm okay now." Darius' gaze shifted to his injured hands, and the shadow of a painful memory crossed his features. "Thank you for rescuing me."

"You don't have to thank me. I was only doing my job. Your family paid us to bring you back."

The boy's expression turned sad, and Carina realized her words sounded harsher than she'd intended, as if she didn't care whether they'd succeeded in their mission. "But I'm glad we found you and got you out of there."

Darius' expression brightened. "When we were stuck in the tunnel, I was scared. I didn't know how we were going to get out. I thought we would die in there. But I didn't mind too much, just so long as I was away from the people who were hurting me."

"But we did get out, right?" said Carina. "And now you're safe. So don't think about that anymore."

There was no stopping the child, however. "You took out your bottle, and you had a drink, and I wanted some because I was so thirsty, but I was too shy to ask."

He seemed hell-bent on going over how they'd ended up at the shuttle. Carina resigned herself to the fact and was grateful that nobody else was around to hear him.

"Then you told me to hold your hand, and you closed your eyes," Darius continued, "and the next thing I knew, we were on the roof next to the starship, and I didn't remember how we got there."

"It doesn't matter how we got there, does it?" Carina asked. "We got where we needed to go. All that matters is that you're safe now."

"I guess so." The boy looked doubtful.

"So let's not talk about it anymore,"

Carina suggested. "It's only going to confuse people. You probably fell asleep while I carried you up to the roof, only you don't remember."

Darius' brow furrowed. "No, I didn't fall asleep. I know how we got there. You cast."

CHAPTER FOURTEEN

Carina almost—but not quite—swallowed the gasp that rose from her throat. The shrewd look on the little boy's face as he watched her reaction told her that she had severely underestimated him.

Though she felt guilty at lying to someone so young, she made another effort to maintain her subterfuge. "What do you mean? We went up to the roof together. Don't you remember going through the vent tunnels?"

The boy giggled. "It's okay. You don't have to pretend with me. I know it's a secret. I won't tell anyone. I promise."

Carina was so deeply conflicted that, for a moment, she was lost for words. Her grandmother's warnings sounded in her mind as strong as ever. She felt an almost physical revulsion at the idea that the boy knew her secret, not least because the only person she'd ever revealed herself to was now dead.

Yet the temptation to speak freely again to another human being about her mage ability was strong. Telling Speidel had been a sweet release after her years of isolation and loneliness.

Adding to her emotional turmoil was a burning curiosity. How did this kid know about casting? Nai Nai had told her that her family were scattered across the galaxy. Could it be possible that this child knew one of her long-lost kin?

She was reclining on pillows, but now she pulled herself upright. "Would you please open the curtains?" she asked the child.

He dutifully hopped down from his seat but then realized he couldn't do as she directed. He held up his thick-gloved hands to her.

"I'm sorry," Carina said. "You sit down. I'll do it."

She got out of bed and, hopping on one leg, she pulled back her bed curtains to the wall, checking that the room was entirely empty and the door was closed.

She returned to her bed, settled herself once more, and looked into the child's eyes.

"Darius, please tell me what you meant by

what you said. How do you think we got to the roof?"

The little boy rolled his eyes. "I already told you. You cast. You drank some elixir, and you closed your eyes, and I guess you thought of the right picture, because after you told me to hold your hand, we went to the roof together. I know that's what happened because I've done it before. I wished so many times I could do that when the bad people were hurting me. Only I didn't have any elixir."

The boy's chin trembled and his eyes swam with tears. Carina reached out and laid her hand on his shoulder.

"You can cast too?" she asked.

Darius nodded, teardrops running down his cheeks. Then suddenly he stopped crying and turned pale. "You aren't going to hurt me, are you? Mother told me I mustn't ever tell anyone what we can do. But you rescued me, and you seem so nice. I thought it would be okay to tell you because you're a mage too, so you know the secret already. You *are* going to take me back to Mother, right? You aren't going to keep me and do bad things to me like the other people did, are you?"

"No one's going to hurt you, Darius," Carina said, "and yes, we are going to take you home. But you and I have to keep this secret between us. Do you understand? You can't tell anyone else what we can do or say anything about casting except when we're alone. Nothing at all. You were very strong and brave to not give any secrets away to the people who hurt you. Can you keep quiet for a little longer? It's very important."

"Sure I can." Darius smiled. "I get it. No one else here knows you're a mage. I can keep your secret as well as mine."

Smart kid. "Thank you." Carina squeezed the boy's shoulder.

Her head was swimming with the implications of what the child had said. She had many questions for him but she didn't know where to start.

"Darius, is everyone in your family a mage?"

"Mother can cast, and Parthenia, Oriana, and Ferne. Castiel and Nahla can't, though, and they hate it," he added, somewhat gleefully.

"Are these people your brothers and sisters?"

"Yep."

"You have five? That's quite a lot. And are you the youngest?"

Darius nodded. He didn't look too happy about his position in the family hierarchy.

"How about your father?" Carina asked. "Can he cast too?"

At the mention of his father, the little

boy's face clouded over. "No, he can't." His lips thinned to a line and he looked angry. Since his father was clearly a sore subject, Carina decided not to continue on that line of questioning. Something else was puzzling her anyway.

"Do you remember how you were kidnapped?" She was wondering how it was that, if Darius had mages in his family, the Dirksens had succeeded in capturing him.

The little boy's face clouded further and his cheeks flushed. His eyes filled with tears again. "It was my fault. I was naughty. Mother told me I must *never leave the garden*." His voice became singsong as he mimicked his mother and wagged a finger at an imaginary Darius. Carina bit back a smile at the adorable imitation.

"She told me that bad people would take me, and she wouldn't be able to get me back because she couldn't give away our secret. But I so wanted to know what was outside. I wanted to see the city and all the different people, and no one would let me go with them. I made a hole in the garden wall and I went out. I was stupid. Outside, everything was boring. There was hardly anyone around, and no trees or flowers or anything like that. I walked away from the house. I was trying to find the city. Not long after, bad people found me. They took me away just like Mother said they would." His head hung low.

"Darius, it's okay," said Carina. "It isn't your fault. Everyone does stupid things every once in a while. You're very little. What happened is the fault of the people who kidnapped you. Besides, we're taking you home now, and you'll see your mother and all your brothers and sisters again. Aren't you glad?"

The child's easy smile quickly returned. "I'm very glad! I can't wait to see them! Except Castiel. I'm not happy that I'll see him. He always teases me. Or...maybe I'm a little bit happy that I'll see him." He finished in a rush, his eyes shining.

Carina was deeply interested in finding out more about the mage members of the Sherrerr family. It sounded like the boy's mother had married a non-mage and had passed on her ability to only some of her children. She wanted to know if there were any more mages among the Sherrerrs, and if they were part of the ancient family or newcomers, but she also wanted to distract Darius from the whole subject.

Now that he knew he was safe, the boy's resolve to keep the family secret had obviously weakened. He'd already brought it up with her, only afterward thinking of the possible consequences. She needed to divert his young mind to other things.

Carina asked Darius to tell her about his home, and a wellspring of information gushed forth from the child's lips. He told her about his bedroom—he had his own and so did all his brothers and sisters—from which he could see the city. He said he hadn't realized how far it was. He also told her about the garden that surrounded the house, which was full of trees as tall as the roof, and lawns where he and his siblings played, and fountains and pools where they cooled down when they were too hot.

The children all had pets they could ride and that would fetch things for them. He described the animals, but Carina didn't recognize any. The pets would climb trees to bring the children fruit when it was ripe. Each child also had his or her own private tutor, who would teach them mathematics, reading, family history, leadership, charm, oration, deportment, and other subjects they would need to run Sherrerr businesses when they grew up. Only Mother taught them to cast, the boy said.

Carina steered him away from the subject of mages again with more questions about his lessons, though the boy clearly thought that was the least interesting aspect of his home life. She noted the comment about casting tuition being left to his mother, however, and filed it away for later reflection.

Darius was in the middle of a delightful impression of his tutor lecturing him about dignity when the doctor returned. "You two aren't still talking? And why are your bed curtains open, Lin? Back to bed with you, young man. That's plenty of chatting for today. The more rest you get, the quicker that gel will work. Come on, off you go." He shooed the little boy back to his own bed.

The child went happily, and Carina also felt better for their conversation. It had lightened the dark shadow that Speidel's death had thrown over her heart.

Whether or not Tarsalan had changed her mind about disbanding the Black Dogs now that they'd fulfilled the assignment, Carina's time with them was over. She knew she wouldn't be able to remain where her memories of the older man were so strong.

Before, she'd had no idea what she could do or where she would go, but Darius' revelation had opened possibilities that Carina could never have imagined.

CHAPTER FIFTEEN

Carina's heart beat fast as, holding Darius' hand, she walked with him from the city toward the Sherrerr estate. Behind them, Tarsalan waited and watched in the shade of a tree at the city outskirts. The Sherrerrs had insisted on a simple handover, much to Tarsalan's apparent chagrin, judging from the bitter tone she used when she informed Carina. Perhaps she'd hoped for a chance to meet members of the powerful clan—an 'in' to the exclusive Sherrerr world.

If an introduction wasn't on the cards, the Black Dogs' owner wasn't going to put herself in any danger by performing the handover. She'd noted the boy's attachment to Carina, however, and had ordered her to accompany him.

Despite the risk that the Dirksens might

launch another attempt to capture the child, Carina wouldn't have had it any other way. This was her chance of a glimpse of Darius' mother, who might be able to tell her much about their mage clan. Carina also clung to a sliver of hope that the woman would be interested in meeting her too, once she heard what Darius had to say.

The Sherrerrs had told Tarsalan they would be watching while Carina brought the boy to them. Did they fear a trick? Carina didn't know. She was only uncomfortably aware of distant eyes on them as they went along. She also felt vulnerable out of her armor and with her face uncovered, as the Sherrerrs had requested. But it couldn't be helped.

They were nearly halfway down the dusty, empty road that led to the vast Sherrerr mansion, having walked around eight hundred meters, when Carina glanced down at Darius and remembered that the child's feet were bare. His toes had healed up, though his toenails hadn't yet regrown, but *Duchess* carried no child-sized shoes and Tarsalan had clearly been so eager to return the child she'd been in too much of a rush to do anything about it.

"Don't your feet hurt?" she asked him.

"Only a little."

"Let me see."

Carina squatted down to look at the soles of Darius' feet. Sure enough, as she'd suspected they were red and blistering. He wasn't a child accustomed to going barefoot.

"Darius," she said, "why didn't you say you were in pain?"

"It doesn't hurt much, and we only have a little way to go now."

Carina tutted. "Hop onto my back." She turned away from the boy and as he climbed onto her, she tucked his legs under her arms. The strange, misshapen shadow of the two of them stretched out long. It was nearing sunset, and the insect life that proliferated in that region had started up its twilight song. Razor-backed beetles the size of small cats crawled out of holes and rubbed their legs along their serrated backs. Carina watched them with interest. She'd always had a thing for bugs.

Feeling the boy's body tense at the sight of one of the beetles flying across their path, Carina reassured him. "Don't worry. They won't hurt you." At least, she was pretty sure they wouldn't. A local had told her they were harmless.

The tall, wide, metallic gates of the Sherrerr estate drew nearer. Carina adjusted the child's weight on her back. She felt no strain carrying him but the movement eased her nerves a little. She scanned the high, blank wall, which glowed yellow in the rays of the setting sun. It was smooth and solid, unmarked by windows or patrolling guards along the top.

Darius wriggled. "Can you go faster, Carina? We're nearly there. I bet Mother is waiting for me at the gatehouse."

"I'm sorry. They told us I had to walk slowly. But it won't be long now."

They had only another couple hundred meters or so to go. Carina turned and looked back to where Tarsalan waited under the tree. The woman was barely visible in its shadow, but she hadn't left. She would wait until she saw the handover take place, she'd said, before returning to the ship. She wouldn't hang around for Carina, who had left *Duchess* for the last time, having said all her goodbyes.

Parting from Stevenson had been particularly hard, and she had the impression that he felt the same, but it couldn't be helped. Her life lay in another direction now, no matter what happened when she returned the Sherrerrs' child.

A clanking sound came from the gate, piercing the insect drone that surrounded them. They were less than a hundred meters from their destination. A small door at the base of the gate opened, and an armed guard came out.

"Stop," he called. "Wait there."

Carina did as he asked. The guard's armor was entirely black, as was his visor. She couldn't make out the man's face at all as he approached. She felt Darius stiffen.

When the Sherrerr guard was twenty meters away he said, "Put the boy down."

Carina squatted down, expecting Darius to slide off her back, but he didn't. He clung tighter. "You have to get down, Darius. This man's going to take you home."

The boy buried his face in the back of her neck. Reaching awkwardly around, she gently extracted him from her back and set him on his feet. His head was down and he crossed his arms defiantly.

"What's wrong?" Carina asked. "Don't you want to see your family again?"

He nodded but didn't raise his head. The guard had reached them, and Darius turned away from him, presenting the man with his hunched over back.

"Come with me, Darius," the guard said, holding out a black-gloved hand.

The boy made a grunt of refusal.

The guard sighed with exasperation. "Give me your hand, Master. You must come with me."

Darius repeated his grunt, adding, "I want Carina to come too. She's a—"

"I can't come with you," Carina

interrupted before the dreaded word could leave the boy's lips. "That wasn't in the instructions, remember?"

The guard's blank visor turned in her direction, and she could feel the man's curious gaze burning into her.

"Please?" Darius asked, lifting his head, his eyes pleading.

"I'm sorry, I can't. But do you remember what we talked about?"

"Oh yes! I forgot." The returned memory lit up the boy's eyes. "Okay, I'll come with you," he said to the guard. Still refusing to take the man's hand, Darius skipped off, heading for home. The guard quickly followed him.

Carina stood and watched Darius the whole way. When he reached the small door, he turned around and gave her a wave. She waved back, smiling at the young boy's happy face. Then the door closed and he was gone.

She looked toward the spot where Tarsalan was waiting and just made out the figure of the woman leaving.

Hugging herself, Carina began what she feared might be a long wait. She went to the side of the road and sat down next to a small boulder. She didn't know how long it would take for Darius to tell his mother about her. She'd made him promise to wait until they were alone together, and that could take a while. The Sherrerrs would probably want to have the boy medically assessed after the joyful reunion, and who knew what else.

Carina passed the time watching the large bugs sing their song and perform their mating dance. She'd been to many worlds in the two years she'd spent as a merc and seen many strange sights. The giant beetles were another to add to her list. She relaxed against the boulder and watched the night's first stars appear.

So many suns, so many planets, she mused. *Life in so many varieties, sapient and non-sapient, vicious and peaceful and everything in between.* In her eighteen years, she'd seen both so much and so little of the galaxy. *Was one of those stars the sun that shone on the home planet of her clan?* Maybe one day she would find it and mages could return from their exile and live together again without fear.

The temperature was dropping fast now that the sun had set. Carina shivered and rubbed her upper arms. The wall to the Sherrerr estate was dark gray, unlit by any external lights. From within the compound arose a glow that had to come from lights within the gardens Darius had mentioned. She imagined the lush grounds, with their trees, shrubs, flowers, and fountains, and the little boy playing happily within them, safely home again.

Darius, have you spoken to your mother yet? Have you told her about me?

The night wore on, and Carina grew colder. The beetles retired to their underground burrows, and silence fell except for the occasional animal noises in the darkness. In the city, movement in the streets diminished. Carina began to think about where she might sleep that night. She had held a faint hope that it might be within the Sherrerr mansion, though that was looking increasingly unlikely.

The garden lights went out. Carina was tired and stiff with cold, and her dreams of companionship with other mages were rapidly fading. It was so dark, she could barely see the road. The Sherrerr estate walls had become black and forbidding.

It was time to leave.

She stood and stretched her aching muscles. Finding the road by feeling with her feet as much as by sight, she began her return to the city. She had her wages from Tarsalan—any bonus for rescuing Darius noticeably absent. She should be able to find a hostel that was still open, and a hot dinner. And then...she would think about that the next day.

It was at that moment that she missed

Speidel the most. What wouldn't she have given for a word of advice from the older man?

The clank of the Sherrerr gate door opening sounded behind her. Carina paused and turned, her defeated heart lifting in hope. Through the gloom, she spotted a guard walking over. Was it the same one who had escorted Darius inside? She couldn't tell.

"You," said the guard. "What's your name?"

"Carina Lin."

"Here, this is for you."

He held out a pouch about the size of a large man's fist. She took it and pulled it open, but in the darkness she couldn't see what was inside.

The guard had already turned to leave.

"Excuse me," Carina said. "Do you have a light I can borrow?"

The man hesitated.

"Please?"

His black visor remained enigmatic, but the guard pulled a small flashlight from his belt, turned it on, and handed it to her.

Carina shone the light into the pouch. A handful of glinting gems were the first items she recognized. They looked valuable. She drew in a breath. The objects that had made her gasp were less impressive than the gems: a tiny transparent box of metal filings, a vial of water, a small container of dust, a firestone, and a bundle of wood splinters tied with a thread: the base ingredients of elixir. Meaningless to an outsider, they were a sign that whoever had sent the pouch knew what she was.

The guard was shifting impatiently. Carina went to hand his flashlight back when its beam caught another item. This one made her knees go weak. It was a simple, almost valueless object, meaningless to an outsider, but to Carina, it meant everything. It was a pebble, polished to a fine shine to bring out its beautiful colors. It was exactly the kind of pebble her grandmother used to sell for a living.

Carina drew the strings on the pouch to close it and returned the flashlight to the guard. "Was there any message?" she asked.

"No. No message. I'd get into town if I were you or you'll be sleeping on the street tonight."

He marched away, leaving her alone in the darkness.

Carina took a final look at the Sherrerr estate. Somewhere inside was a mage who wished her well. Perhaps it was even someone who had known Nai Nai and understood her connection with the woman, but for some reason would not or could not talk to her.

For now, the Sherrerr fortress was impregnable and she couldn't see a way to change that, but in a way she didn't care. Carina was no longer alone.

Carina's story continues in...

DAUGHTER OF DISCORD

STAR MAGE SAGA BOOK 1

Thanks for reading!

Reviews are very important to the success of a book. If you enjoyed *Star Mage Exile*, please consider leaving an honest review. Even a few sentences help.

Sign up to my reader group for free books, discounts on new releases, review team invitations and other interesting stuff:

https://jjgreenauthor.com/

ALSO BY J.J. GREEN

SHADOWS OF THE VOID SERIES

SPACE COLONY ONE SERIES

*CARRIE HATCHETT, SPACE
ADVENTURER SERIES*

LOST TO TOMORROW

THERE COMES A TIME
A SCIENCE FICTION
COLLECTION

DAWN FALCON
A FANTASY COLLECTION